JOHN STEINBECK

The Moon is Down

With an Introduction by Donald V. Coers

PENGUIN BOOKS

PENGUIN BOOKS

Published by the Penguin Group
Penguin Books Ltd, 80 Strand, London WC2R 0RL, England
Penguin Putnam Inc., 375 Hudson Street, New York, New York 10014, USA
Penguin Books Australia Ltd, 250 Camberwell Road, Camberwell, Victoria 3124, Australia
Penguin Books Canada Ltd, 10 Alcorn Avenue, Toronto, Ontario, Canada M4V 3B2
Penguin Books India (P) Ltd, 11 Community Centre, Panchsheel Park, New Delhi – 110 017, India
Penguin Books (NZ) Ltd, Cnr Rosedale and Airborne Roads, Albany, Auckland, New Zealand
Penguin Books (South Africa) (Pty) Ltd, 24 Sturdee Avenue, Rosebank 2196, South Africa

Penguin Books Ltd, Registered Offices: 80 Strand, London WC2R 0RL, England

www.penguin.com

First published in the United States of America by The Viking Press 1942
Published in a Viking Compass Edition 1970
Published in Penguin Books 1982
This edition with an introduction by Donald V. Coers
published in Penguin Books 1995
Reprinted in Penguin Classics 2000
8

Printed in England by Clays Ltd, St Ives plc
Set in Bembo

CONTENTS

INTRODUCTION

By the summer of 1940, a little more than a year after the publication of *The Grapes of Wrath,* the Nazis had engulfed much of Europe. John Steinbeck was by then a world-class author. He was also both a clear-eyed political realist who understood that U.S. involvement in the war was inevitable, and a patriot eager to contribute to the Allies' cause. That spring he had been in Mexico writing the screenplay for *The Forgotten Village,* and he had been troubled because it seemed to him that in Latin America the Nazis were outclassing the Allies in propaganda. He was so concerned, in fact, that on June 26, four days after France signed an armistice with Germany, he met with President Roosevelt to discuss the problem. There is no record to indicate that the president took any advice Steinbeck may have offered, but the writer's enthusiasm for fighting fascism was not dampened. Over the next two or three years he served voluntarily in several of the government intelligence and information agencies created between 1940 and 1942.

Two of the organizations Steinbeck worked for were precursors of the CIA: the Office of Coordinator of Information (COI) and the Office of Strategic Services (OSS). Both were headed by Colonel William J. "Wild Bill" Donovan, a Republican New York lawyer who was awarded the Congressional Medal of Honor during the First World War. Despite his political conservatism, Donovan was an open-minded administrator who encouraged fresh ideas and was willing to employ unorthodox techniques and outré people to achieve his goals. He was also particularly interested in civilian morale and, consequently, in propaganda.

While Steinbeck was working for the COI, probably in

midsummer of 1941, he and Donovan discussed the idea that Steinbeck might write a work of propaganda. At the same time, Steinbeck's duties at COI brought him into contact with displaced citizens from the recently occupied countries of Europe, among them Norway and Denmark (invaded in April of 1940), and France, Belgium, and the Netherlands (overrun in May and June). The refugees intrigued Steinbeck with stories about the activities of underground resistance movements in their native lands. Over twenty years later Steinbeck recounted in an article entitled "Reflections on a Lunar Eclipse" how the exiles' information helped him decide what kind of propaganda he would write.

> The experiences of the victim nations, while they differed in some degree with national psychologies, had many things in common. At the time of invasion there had been confusion; in some of the nations there were secret Nazi parties, there were spies and turncoats. [The Norwegian Nazi, Vidkun] Quisling has left his name as a synonym for traitor. Then there were collaborators, some moved by fear and others simply for advancement and profit. Finally there were the restrictive measures of the Germans, their harsh demands and savage punishments. All of these factors had to be correlated and understood before an underground movement could form and begin to take action.

By September 1941 Steinbeck had decided to write a work of fiction using what he had learned about the psychological effects of enemy occupation upon the populace of conquered nations. Because he "did not believe people are very different in essentials," he originally set his story in America:

> I wrote my fictional account about a medium-sized American town with its countryside of a kind I knew well. There

would be collaborators certainly. Don't forget the Bund
meetings in our cities, the pro-German broadcasts before the
war and the kind of man who loves any success: "Mussolini
made the trains run on time." "Hitler saved Germany from
communism." It was not beyond reason that our town
would have its cowards, its citizens who sold out for profit.
But under this, I did and do believe, would be the hard core
that could not be defeated. And so I wrote my account bas-
ing its fiction on facts extracted from towns already under
the Nazi heel.

Steinbeck submitted his "fictional account" for approval
to another of Donovan's agencies, the Foreign Information
Service. Officials there rejected it because they feared that
postulating an American defeat might be demoralizing.
Steinbeck's refugee friends, certain that his story would boost
morale in their already occupied homelands, urged him to
circumvent official objections by shifting the setting. He
took their advice and placed the story in an unnamed country, "cold and stern like Norway, cunning and implacable
like Denmark, reasonable like France."

Steinbeck finished his revised version just in time for Pearl
Harbor, and Viking Press published it as a short novel, *The
Moon Is Down*, in early March of 1942. The next month it
played on Broadway, and a year later premiered as a movie.
Its title comes from the beginning of act 2 of *Macbeth*. Just
before Banquo and Fleance encounter Macbeth on his way
to murder Duncan, Banquo asks his son, "How goes the
night, boy?" Fleance replies, "The moon is down; I have
not heard the clock," foreshadowing the descent of evil on
the kingdom. Steinbeck's allusion suggests that the Nazis had
brought a similar spiritual darkness to Europe.

The Moon Is Down appeared in bookstores during the
bleakest days of the war for the United States. While Americans reeled from Pearl Harbor, the Japanese overran much

of Southeast Asia and seized strategic islands dotting vast expanses of the Pacific Ocean until they were poised within striking distance of the northern coast of Australia. The Doolittle raids, America's first flicker of hope, were still a month away, and it would be three months before the first Japanese defeat, the Battle of Midway. The picture looked equally grim for America's allies in Europe. Hitler's crushing offenses continued unchecked, and the first shots in the watershed Battle of Stalingrad would not be fired for another nine or ten months. As U.S. factories frenetically retooled from consumer goods to war matériel, German U-boats lurked along the Gulf and Atlantic coasts, sinking Allied ships faster than they could be replaced and threatening supply lines to Britain. The Allies' great fear in March 1942 was that they might not be able to hold out long enough for American troops and industrial might to help reverse the course of the war.

Understandably, when *The Moon Is Down* came out late that dreary winter, the critics were more interested in predicting its potential as propaganda than in weighing its merits as literature. But Steinbeck's method was far subtler than that of the overcooked rant customarily served up in this country at the time. His anonymous setting, for instance, is simply a peace-loving country, very much like Norway, which is invaded suddenly and without provocation by a much stronger neighbor, very much like Germany. To be sure, Steinbeck leaves no doubt whom he has in mind. Officers in the invading army allude to "the Leader" of their homeland and to his bringing a "new order" to Europe. There is a reference to the Leader's country's having fought Belgium and France twenty years earlier—an unsubtle reminder of Germany's repeat performance in the European theater. Beyond such hints, Steinbeck refused to adopt the contemporary Teutonic stereotypes. There are no heel-clicking Huns, no depraved, monocled intellectuals, no thundering *sieg heils* in his fable-like tale. Instead, Steinbeck depicts his putative Germans as human beings with normal feelings. They offer the citizens of the conquered country justifications for their invasion. They plead for understanding. They miss their families. They want their victims to accept them. Yet nothing can disguise their theft of freedom, and eventually the local patriots' desire to regain it impels them to resist. The militarily superior invaders retaliate, but the impression remains that ultimately the patriots will prevail because a society of free individuals is stronger in the long run than a totalitarian power dependent on herd men. In the mayor's words, "It is always the herd men who win battles and the free men who win wars."

Steinbeck's affirmative, toned-down approach to propaganda in *The Moon Is Down* touched off the fiercest literary battle of the Second World War. Many critics liked the novel, but some did not, and their number included such formidable names as Clifton Fadiman and James Thurber. In effect, the detractors accused Steinbeck of naïveté. The creator of the savvy, muscular realism of *The Grapes of Wrath* was now being soft on the Nazis by depicting them as human beings and by infusing his story with a fuzzy, fairy-tale atmosphere. Doubtless well-intentioned but poorly conceived, Steinbeck's propaganda would surely demoralize the victims of Nazi aggression in occupied Europe—the very people he wanted to help. The proper way to raise a fighting spirit among a brutalized populace, one critic intoned, was with hard-hitting hype bearing a title like "Guts in the Mud," not with "soft and dreamy" stuff like *The Moon Is Down*.

The controversy raged for months in major newspapers and magazines—most prominently *The New York Times*, the *Herald Tribune*, *The New Yorker*, *The New Republic*, and the *Saturday Review*. To be sure, *The Moon Is Down* had its defenders. In fact, more critics praised than criticized it. But the attacks blindsided Steinbeck. For years he had been praised as a skilled artist with socially enlightened views—a proletarian writer with polish. Suddenly he found himself savaged for a well-meaning contribution to the war effort. The criticism was corrosive, calling into question not only his artistic instincts, but, far worse, his political acumen, his credentials as an antifascist, and his very patriotism. Steinbeck was wounded, and his wounds were still tender over ten years later when he referred sarcastically to his detractors, chiefly Fadiman and Thurber, in an essay entitled "My Short Novels."

> The war came on, and I wrote *The Moon Is Down* as a kind of celebration of the durability of democracy. I couldn't conceive that the book would be denounced. I had written of Germans as men, not supermen, and this was considered a very weak attitude to take. I couldn't make much sense out of this, and it seems absurd now that we know the Germans were men, and thus fallible, even defeatable. It was said that I didn't know anything about war, and this was perfectly true, though how Park Avenue commandos found me out I can't conceive.

The debate died long before the war ended, and after the war the political and philosophical issues it had spawned were moot. There were early indications that, as Steinbeck had intended, *The Moon Is Down* had found a receptive audience in Nazi-occupied Europe. King Haakon VII gave him a medal honoring the novel's influence in Norway, and European scholars occasionally mentioned its wartime popularity, but for nearly a half century the supporting details remained scattered and anecdotal. No one knew how effective Steinbeck's contribution had been.

Over the last few years new evidence has emerged that

documents the extraordinarily positive reception of *The Moon Is Down* in Nazi-occupied Western Europe, and confirms the novel's success as propaganda. Throughout Norway, Denmark, Holland, and France, it was translated, printed on clandestine presses, and distributed, sometimes under the very nose of the Gestapo. The underground operations involved lawyers, book dealers, retired military personnel, housewives, businesspeople, students, and teachers who took great risks to disseminate *The Moon Is Down* because it spoke so directly to them and to their situation and so persuasively supported their cause. Their explanations of its effectiveness are remarkably similar: Somehow an author living thousands of miles away in a land of peace sensed precisely how they felt as victims of Nazi aggression. It never occurred to them that the novel was sympathetic to their enemy. In fact, they regarded it as far more effective than the prevailing formula propaganda, which struck them as comical because it was so absurdly exaggerated. And the Nazis certainly did not think the novel treated them favorably. They banned it wherever they were in control. A member of the resistance in Italy reported that mere possession of it meant an automatic death sentence.

In spite of the Nazis' efforts to suppress *The Moon Is Down,* hundreds of thousands of copies of the Norwegian, Danish, Dutch, and French clandestine editions circulated during the occupation. It was easily the most popular work of propaganda in occupied Western Europe. The efforts put forth by the resistance and by ordinary citizens to distribute the novel within their respective countries, and the risks they took in doing so, bear witness to the importance they attached to it.

The illegal Norwegian-language edition of *The Moon Is Down* was translated in Sweden by a forty-year-old exile named Nils Lie. Before the invasion of his homeland, Lie had been chief consultant for Gyldendal Publishers. Gyldendal had brought out translations of *Tortilla Flat, Of Mice and Men,* and *The Grapes of Wrath* in 1938, 1939, and 1940, respectively. Late in 1942, several thousand copies of Lie's translation of *The Moon Is Down* were printed by a Swedish press on tissue-thin paper, bound with soft covers, and smuggled into Norway. Some were spirited across isolated points along the thousand-mile border between Sweden and Norway, and a few were dropped from airplanes, but the bulk were cached in luggage carried by regular rail lines. Most of the small, easily concealed pamphlet editions got past the control stations; apparently, a few did not, because officials in the Nazi puppet government in Norway were almost immediately aware of the existence of the special translation. They were so uneasy about its possible effects on the Norwegian people that, in December, when thirty-six copies were confiscated in courier luggage shipped to Oslo from Sweden, six were sent immediately to the head of the state police and to the president of the puppet government himself—the infamous Quisling. Thousands of unconfiscated copies were delivered by the Norwegian resistance to reliable citizens, who passed them along to friends. Frits von der Lippe, a wartime employee at Gyldendal in Oslo, related nearly forty years later how he became a typical "distributor" of the novel:

> An astonishing thing happened [to me] in 1943. In the middle of the day in Oslo's main thoroughfare, Karl Johan Street, among uniformed people and civilians who might be dangerous, a man came up on the side of me and said, whispering, "Follow me. I have something for you. Something you shall distribute." I knew the face, but not the name. I said to him, "Why here, now?" He said, "I came this morning, and I leave tonight, when I have delivered what I have in the suitcase." "Back to Sweden?" I said. "Yes." Then we

went from Karl Johan over to Stortengade, the next street, and went into a house with an elevator with seven stops and traveled up and down, up and down, until we were alone. Then this man gave me four or five packages and said, "Go straight home." And he put me out on the fifth stop and went down the elevator, and I've not seen him since. I went home and opened up one of the small packages and found the small copies of *Natt uten måne* [the Norwegian title of *The Moon Is Down*].

Such was the popularity of *The Moon Is Down* in Norway during the occupation that in the middle of June of 1945, just five weeks after the liberation, a new legal edition was in bookstores. At that time in Norway an average printing for a novel was between one thousand and two thousand copies. *The Moon Is Down* came out in two printings of ten thousand copies each, both of which quickly sold out. The play version was performed immediately after the Oslo national theater reopened, only four months after the liberation. A Norwegian critic hailed *The Moon Is Down* as "the epic of the Norwegian underground."

A uniquely qualified witness to the novel's effectiveness as propaganda in Norway was William Colby, later director of the Central Intelligence Agency under two presidents, Nixon and Ford. One of the few Americans on the scene during the occupation, Colby served during the early spring of 1945 in a special operations unit of ski paratroopers attached to the Office of Strategic Services. He had read *The Moon Is Down* three years earlier and was "tremendously impressed" by how well Steinbeck had captured the Norwegian national mood.

In occupied Denmark, the first illegal Danish-language edition of *The Moon Is Down* was translated by two young law students, Jørgen Jacobsen and Paul Lang. They had received a copy of the American edition shortly before Christmas of 1942, along with a request for a Danish translation from a student resistance group known simply as the Danish Students. Its members hoped that distribution of the novel in Denmark would embolden the resistance movement there. Jacobsen and Lang completed their translation in one week. They worked day and night with a concise *Oxford English Dictionary* in one hand and a glass of beer in the other, glancing over their shoulders for the Gestapo. An anonymous comrade in the Danish Students delivered it to another member for printing. A short time after that, other printers with connections to the student resistance were assembling separate clandestine editions of Jacobsen and Lang's translation. Perhaps the most productive of these printers was Mogens Staffeldt, a Copenhagen bookseller then in his late twenties who had been involved in resistance activities from the day the Germans invaded his country. Staffeldt hocked his life insurance policy to buy the mimeograph machine he used to crank out copies of *The Moon Is Down* in his bookstore. That bookstore, located on the town square, was on the bottom floor of the building which housed Gestapo headquarters for Copenhagen. But the steady traffic of Gestapo entering and leaving the building twenty-four hours a day failed to slow Staffeldt's operations. At the time, the Nazis regarded Denmark as a "model protectorate" and were eager to mollify its citizenry. Staffeldt turned that attitude to his advantage. On several occasions when loyal Danish students came to his bookstore to pick up disguised bundles of *The Moon Is Down* and other forbidden titles for delivery to various distribution centers, Staffeldt stepped out of his store, summoned passing Gestapo officers, and enlisted their aid in loading the anti-Nazi literature. "Don't just stand there," he would scold; "help these kids!" The enemy's secret police invariably responded by scrambling about in unwitting service to the Danish resistance.

Staffeldt alone mimeographed fifteen thousand copies of *The Moon Is Down*. The Danish students delivered them to reliable contacts in other bookshops or in large businesses such as banks or shipping firms. These contacts in turn sold them to trusted customers or employees. The proceeds went to the resistance. Eventually the translation was in such demand that many citizens retyped it and ran off new mimeograph editions for further circulation among their friends. Each mimeograph master yielded a limited number of copies, so the entire novel had to be retyped again and again. Later in the occupation another Danish translation with a different title appeared. It too was widely distributed.

As in Norway, the appeal of *The Moon Is Down* in occupied Denmark was attested to after the war ended by the immediate publication of a regular trade edition. The first run was of five thousand copies. That was followed by a second printing of eight thousand copies in 1961, a third of ten thousand in 1962, and additional printings in 1974, 1976, and 1980—remarkable quantities for a country whose population today is only five million.

The illegal Dutch-language version of *The Moon Is Down* was prepared by Ferdinand Sterneberg, who was a forty-three-year-old actor living in Amsterdam when the Nazis overran his country in May of 1940. Early in 1944 a friend with ties to an underground publishing firm known as De Bizige Bij (the Busy Bee) brought him an English-language edition and asked him to translate it. Sterneberg, a longtime admirer of Steinbeck, agreed. The Busy Bee edition came out later that year in a run of over one thousand copies. These sold at a high price—today roughly equivalent to between two and three hundred dollars apiece—because the proceeds were directed to a resistance organization providing relief for actors and actresses thrown out of work for refusing to join the Nazi-sponsored cultural guild.

Sterneberg, who used the nom de guerre Tjebbo Hemelrijk, also prepared a Dutch-language stage version of *The Moon Is Down,* from which he gave dramatic readings in Amsterdam, in The Hague, and in the countryside. According to Sterneberg, he presented his one-man show to audiences of between twenty-five and fifty people, whom he always prepared for the possibility of a Gestapo raid. Immediately before and after these readings Sterneberg and his friends sold copies of his translation. After more than fifty performances he was forced to quit. He had been hiding in his apartment two Jewish friends, a brother and sister. They lived with him throughout the occupation, and escaped discovery during those years only because of meticulous precautions. "Untrustworthy" neighbors lived in the apartment below, so Sterneberg's friends could not move around, use the bathroom, draw water, or even talk when he was gone. Sterneberg could not in good conscience continue leaving them in such danger and discomfort for the long periods of absence his readings required.

After the war Sterneberg and his fellow actors gave many performances of the dramatic version of *The Moon Is Down.* The Busy Bee also brought out a new edition of the novel. Ironically, because the publishers had access to better quality paper during the war than immediately following the liberation, the new edition was inferior to the one published secretly during the occupation. Several fine Dutch editions have been published since.

The French clandestine edition of *The Moon Is Down* was released in February 1944, six months before the liberation of Paris. Its printing of fifteen hundred copies was the largest of the entire war undertaken by a Parisian underground press aptly named Éditions de Minuit (Midnight Editions). The translation was by Yvonne Paraf, a young woman who had adopted the nom de guerre Yvonne Desvignes. She was a childhood friend of the printer for Midnight Editions. Paraf worked from an English-language edition of *The Moon Is Down* published two years earlier in Sweden. She knew that a French translation had already been published in Switzerland in 1943, but she and other members of the French resistance wanted a new one, because Swiss officials had censored passages that might have offended the Germans. The Swiss had deleted Steinbeck's references to England, to the war in Russia, and to the occupation of Belgium by the invading army of the same country that had occupied it twenty years previously, all of which served indirectly to identify the unnamed country to which that army belonged. At that time the Swiss felt vulnerable to German invasion and were trying hard to avoid displeasing their powerful neighbor.

In France, as in Denmark and Holland, sales of illegal editions of *The Moon Is Down* helped fund the resistance. The money earned by Paraf's translation was turned over to the National Committee of Writers, which used it to support the families of patriotic printers and typographers shot or deported by the Nazis. According to the French patriotic press, the impact of *The Moon Is Down* in occupied France was "immense and incontestable." Immediately after liberation, Midnight Editions published the novel in a volume identical in every detail to the clandestine version. It was included, in fact, as one of several works in a special collection constituting Midnight Editions' first public issue. The single printing of *The Moon Is Down* was of 5,325 numbered copies.

The Moon Is Down also enjoyed unusual popularity in European countries that escaped German occupation. The expurgated French-language Swiss edition mentioned earlier was published in Lausanne in 1943 by Marguerat. A German-language Swiss edition appeared in Zurich the same year, published by Humanitas Verlag. Theaters in Basel performed the play version to enthusiastic audiences, and then the Schauspielhaus in Zurich produced a highly acclaimed run of approximately two hundred performances. In England, Heinemann published its first edition of the novel in 1942, following with a so-called "Middle East Edition" the next year. The English Theater Guild published the dramatic version in 1943, the same year the play opened at London's Whitehall Theatre. The Swedes brought out two editions in 1942 besides the one intended for distribution by the resistance in Norway: a Swedish translation published by Bonniers and an English-language version printed by the Continental Book Company—the edition Paraf used for her French translation. Soviet magazines serialized two different Russian translations of the novel in 1943: a complete version published in *Znamya,* and excerpts in *Ogonyok.* Despite the virtually unanimous disapproval of Soviet critics, who regarded it as vague and unrealistic, *The Moon Is Down* was the best-known work of American literature in the Soviet Union during the war.

There is also evidence that the novel was distributed within the Axis itself. During a visit to Florence more than a decade after the war ended, Steinbeck was approached by an Italian who had opposed Mussolini. He had translated *The Moon Is Down,* mimeographed five hundred copies, and then circulated them among fellow members of the resistance. They had been in great demand.

The Nazis were not the only fascists against whom *The Moon Is Down* served effectively as propaganda. Far to the east, a well-known Chinese professor of literature, Chien Gochuen, had obtained a copy of an English edition through the office of the British press attaché in Chongqing, China's wartime capital. Chien recognized immediately its potential propaganda value for his country, much of it then occupied by the Japanese. He completed his translation in 1942, and beginning early the next year it ran as installments under Chien's nom de guerre, Ch'in Ko Chuan, in the first seven issues of *New China* magazine. Ten thousand copies of each of those issues were published—a remarkable number given the formidable wartime shortages in China. Shortly after the last of the installments appeared, the publishers compiled them in a single edition for circulation throughout China. Forty years later, a spokesman for the book company that published *New China* magazine remembered that the Chinese people were encouraged by "the patriotic eagerness of [Steinbeck's] characters to resist their conquerors."

Today, at a half century's distance from the controversy ignited by the publication of *The Moon Is Down,* it is clear that Fadiman, Thurber, and other critics who had prophesied its failure as propaganda were entirely wrong. Evidence of its success in Nazi-occupied Europe and in China is compelling: the dedication of those who translated, printed, and distributed it at considerable risk; the impressive number of editions and copies published—during the occupation, on makeshift machinery and under taxing conditions, as well as after the war by recently liberated publishing houses; and the accounts of former members of the resistance and others who witnessed firsthand the force of its ideas.

But beyond the obvious conclusion that Steinbeck was right and his critics wrong about what would constitute effective propaganda, several questions arise. Why were the hostile American critics so mistaken, and how do we account for the difference between their reaction and that of the Europeans? Why did the American detractors fail to appreciate what so appealed to the Europeans? And finally, what does the stunning wartime European reception of *The Moon Is Down* tell us about the genius of John Steinbeck?

The French writer and philosopher Jean-Paul Sartre offers a theory that probably accounts for the critics' divergence of opinion. In his postwar essay *What Is Literature?* he contends that we can have no true understanding of a literary work unless we know who an author is writing for. To illustrate his point, Sartre recalls a wartime literary controversy similar to that surrounding *The Moon Is Down*. Another highly popular work of anti-Nazi fiction published in France during the war was a short novel entitled *The Silence of the Sea*, written by Jean Bruller, a member of the French resistance better known by his nom de guerre, Vercors. Like Steinbeck, Bruller portrayed the Germans as human beings, often intelligent, if misguided, and frequently polite and likable. *The Silence of the Sea* succeeded as propaganda within occupied France, but it found a hostile audience in French men and women living abroad, many of whom in fact accused Bruller of collaboration. Sartre's explanation for the mixed reception is that Bruller was writing for compatriots living under the Nazis. He was among them, sharing their feelings and the routines of their existence. He realized that to stereotype all Germans as ogres would have been laughable to those who had daily contact with the enemy and who knew better.

Like Bruller, Steinbeck revealed in his approach to propaganda not only a shrewd psychological perception of what would work and what would not, but also a respect for his European audience. The crude oversimplifications of most propaganda are, after all, patronizing. There is no such condescension in Steinbeck's approach. But Steinbeck's understanding of what would appeal to a European audience under the unusual conditions of the day is all the more remarkable because, unlike Bruller, who had the advantage of being on the scene and of writing about people he knew well, Steinbeck was a foreigner living thousands of miles away.

Steinbeck's own explanation for the perceptiveness that

made his propaganda so effective is simple. During his visit to Norway in 1946 to receive King Haakon's medal, he was asked on several occasions how he knew so well what the resistance there was doing. His answer was, "I put myself in your place and thought what I would do." That reply explains more than the success of *The Moon Is Down* in occupied Europe; it reminds us what readers of Steinbeck all over the world had already recognized as among the writer's major attributes: his sure sense of audience, and his empathy with the oppressed. European partisans who ran considerable risk to publish and distribute *The Moon Is Down* because they believed it would help their cause agreed about the source of its power: a Danish publisher ascribed it to "Steinbeck's sincere sentiment . . . a human quality which penetrates"; a Norwegian reviewer to his ability to capture "our feelings . . . our problems, our hopes, our sorrows"; the Dutch translator to Steinbeck's insight, "especially into [our] reaction against the ones who took over the country"; and the French translator to the author's masterful understanding. All are acknowledgments of the sympathy and the social intuition that John Steinbeck had already demonstrated in works of the middle and late 1930s, most notably *Of Mice and Men, In Dubious Battle,* and *The Grapes of Wrath*. The success of *The Moon Is Down* as propaganda, then, underscores Steinbeck's signal literary strengths.

Most works of propaganda do not survive the crises that produce them. *The Moon Is Down* is an exception. Since 1945 it has appeared in at least ninety-two editions in the United States, England, Denmark, Norway, the Netherlands, Spain, Mexico, Hungary, France, Belgium, Turkey, Germany, Switzerland, pre-Communist Mainland China, Taiwan, Japan, Egypt, Sweden, Italy, Portugal, Brazil, Korea, India, Greece, Iran, Poland, Czechoslovakia, and Burma. The novel's endurance suggests that while *The Moon*

Is Down may have been conceived, written, and used as propaganda, it is probably best described as a work of literature that served as propaganda. Judged by purely artistic standards, it is not among the author's best efforts. Scholars and reviewers have most frequently criticized its wooden characters and transparent didacticism, flaws characteristic of novels of ideas. But few literary works in our time have demonstrated so triumphantly the power of ideas in the face of cold steel and brute force, and few have spoken so reassuringly to so many people of different countries and cultures. Against the fiercest assault on freedom during this century, John Steinbeck calmly reaffirmed in *The Moon Is Down* the bedrock principles of democracy: the worth of the individual, and the power deriving from free citizens sharing common commitments.

SUGGESTIONS FOR
FURTHER READING

PRIMARY WORKS BY JOHN STEINBECK

"About Ed Ricketts." In John Steinbeck and Ed Ricketts, *The Log from the* Sea of Cortez. New York: Viking Press, 1951.

"Letters to Alicia." *Weekend with Newsday*, December 11, 1965, 3W.

The Moon Is Down: Play in Two Parts. New York: Dramatists Play Service, 1942.

"My Short Novels." *Steinbeck and His Critics*, edited by E. W. Tedlock, Jr., and C. V. Wicker. Albuquerque: University of New Mexico Press, 1957, 38–40.

"Reflections on a Lunar Eclipse." *Herald Tribune* (New York) *Book Week*, October 6, 1963, 3.

Steinbeck: A Life in Letters. Edited by Elaine Steinbeck and Robert Wallsten. New York: Viking Press, 1975.

SECONDARY SOURCES

BOOKS

Astro, Richard. *John Steinbeck and Edward F. Ricketts: The Shaping of a Novelist*. Minneapolis: University of Minnesota Press, 1973.

Benson, Jackson J. *Looking for Steinbeck's Ghost*. Norman: University of Oklahoma Press, 1988.

———. *The True Adventures of John Steinbeck, Writer*. New York: Viking Press, 1984.

Brown, Anthony Cave. *The Last Hero: Wild Bill Donovan*. New York: Times Books, 1982.

Coers, Donald V. *John Steinbeck as Propagandist:* The Moon Is Down *Goes to War*. Tuscaloosa: University of Alabama Press, 1991.

Debû-Bridel, Jacques. *Les Éditions de Minuit: Historique et bibliographie*. Paris: Éditions de Minuit, 1945.

Fontenrose, Joseph. *John Steinbeck: An Introduction and Interpretation*. New York: Barnes and Noble, 1963.

French, Warren. *John Steinbeck's Fiction Revisited*. New York: Twayne Publishers, 1994.

Goldstone, Adrian H., and John R. Payne. *John Steinbeck: A Bibliographical Catalogue of the Adrian H. Goldstone Collection*. Austin: University of Texas Humanities Research Center, 1974.

Hæstrup, Jørgen. *From Occupied to Ally: Danish Resistance Movement, 1940–45*. Translated by Reginald Spink. Copenhagen: Det Berlingske Bogtrykkeri, 1963.

Hayashi, Tetsumaro. The Moon Is Down: *Three Explications*. Steinbeck's World War II Fiction, no. 1. Muncie, Ind.: Steinbeck Research Institute, Ball State University, 1986.

Lampe, David. *The Savage Canary: The Story of the Resistance in Denmark*. London: Cassell, 1957.

Levant, Howard. *The Novels of John Steinbeck: A Critical Study*. Columbia: University of Missouri Press, 1974.

Lisca, Peter. *The Wide World of John Steinbeck*. New Brunswick: Rutgers University Press, 1958.

Marks, Lester. *Thematic Design in the Novels of John Steinbeck*. The Hague: Mouton, 1969.

McCarthy, Paul. *John Steinbeck*. New York: Frederick Ungar, 1979.

Millichap, Joseph R. *Steinbeck and Film*. New York: Frederick Ungar, 1983.

Parini, Jay. *John Steinbeck: A Biography*. New York: Henry Holt, 1995.

Petrow, Richard. *The Bitter Years: The Invasion and Occupation of Denmark and Norway, April 1940–May 1945*. New York: Morrow, 1974.

Sartre, Jean-Paul. *What Is Literature?* Translated by Bernard Frechtman. New York: Philosophical Library, 1949.

Timmerman, John H. *John Steinbeck's Fiction: The Aesthetics of the Road Taken*. Norman: University of Oklahoma Press, 1986.

ARTICLES

Benson, Jackson J. "Through a Political Glass, Darkly: The Example of John Steinbeck." *Studies in American Fiction*, Spring 1984, 45–59.

Clancy, Charles J. *"The Moon Is Down."* In *A Study Guide to Steinbeck*, part 2, edited by Tetsumaro Hayashi. Metuchen, New Jersey: Scarecrow Press, 1979.

Coers, Donald V. " 'John Believed in *Man*': An Interview with Mrs. John Steinbeck." In *After* The Grapes of Wrath: *Essays on John Steinbeck in Honor of Tetsumaro Hayashi*, edited by Donald V. Coers, Paul D. Ruffin, and Robert J. DeMott. Athens: Ohio University Press, 1995.

Ditsky, John. "Steinbeck's 'European' Play-Novella: *The Moon Is Down*." *Steinbeck Quarterly*, Winter–Spring 1987, 9–18. Reprinted in *The Short Novels of John Steinbeck*, edited by Jackson J. Benson. Durham: Duke University Press, 1990.

French, Warren. "*The Moon Is Down:* John Steinbeck's 'Times.' " *Steinbeck Quarterly*, Summer–Fall 1978, 77–87.

Hyman, Stanley Edgar. "Some Notes on John Steinbeck." *Antioch Review*, June 1942. Reprinted in *Steinbeck and His Critics*, edited by E. W. Tedlock, Jr., and C. V. Wicker. Albuquerque: University of New Mexico Press, 1957.

Lewis, Cliff. "Art for Politics: John Steinbeck and FDR." In *After* The Grapes of Wrath: *Essays on John Steinbeck in Honor of Tetsumaro Hayashi*, edited by Donald V. Coers, Paul D. Ruffin, and Robert J. DeMott. Athens: Ohio University Press, 1995.

Morsberger, Robert E. "Steinbeck's War." In *The Steinbeck Question: New Essays in Criticism*, edited by Donald R. Noble. Troy, NY: Whitson Publishing Company, 1993.

Sartre, Jean-Paul. "American Novelists in French Eyes." *Atlantic Monthly*, August 1946, 114–18.

Schulberg, Budd. "John Steinbeck: A Lion in Winter." In *The Four Seasons of Success*. Garden City, N.Y.: Doubleday, 1972. Reprinted in *Conversations with John Steinbeck*, edited by Thomas Fensch. Jackson: University Press of Mississippi, 1988.

Shiraga, Eiko. "Three Strong Women in Steinbeck's *The Moon Is*

Down." In *After* The Grapes of Wrath: *Essays on John Steinbeck in Honor of Tetsumaro Hayashi*, edited by Donald V. Coers, Paul D. Ruffin, and Robert J. DeMott. Athens: Ohio University Press, 1995.

Simmonds, Roy S. "The Metamorphosis of *The Moon Is Down*, March 1942–March 1943." In *After* The Grapes of Wrath: *Essays on John Steinbeck in Honor of Tetsumaro Hayashi*, edited by Donald V. Coers, Paul D. Ruffin, and Robert J. DeMott. Athens: Ohio University Press, 1995.

———. "Steinbeck and World War II: The Moon Goes Down." *Steinbeck Quarterly*, Winter–Spring 1984, 14–34.

Weeks, Donald. "Steinbeck against Steinbeck." *Pacific Spectator*, Autumn 1947. Reprinted in *John Steinbeck*, edited by Harold Bloom. New York: Chelsea House Publishers, 1987.

THE MOON IS DOWN

1

By ten-forty-five it was all over. The town was occupied, the defenders defeated, and the war finished. The invader had prepared for this campaign as carefully as he had for larger ones. On this Sunday morning the postman and the policeman had gone fishing in the boat of Mr. Corell, the popular storekeeper. He had lent them his trim sailboat for the day. The postman and the policeman were several miles at sea when they saw the small, dark transport, loaded with soldiers, go quietly past them. As officials of the town, this was definitely their business, and these two put about, but of course the battalion was in possession by the time they could make port. The policeman and the postman could not even get into their own offices in the Town Hall, and when they insisted on their rights they were taken prisoners of war and locked up in the town jail.

The local troops, all twelve of them, had been away, too, on this Sunday morning, for Mr. Corell, the popular store-keeper, had donated lunch, targets, cartridges, and prizes for a shooting-competition to take place six miles back in the hills, in a lovely glade Mr. Corell owned. The local troops, big, loose-hung boys, heard the planes and in the distance saw the parachutes, and they came back to town at double-quick step. When they arrived, the invader had flanked the road with machine guns. The loose-hung soldiers, having very little experience in war and none at all in defeat, opened fire with their rifles. The machine guns clattered for a moment and six of the soldiers became dead riddled bundles and three half-dead riddled bundles, and three of the soldiers escaped into the hills with their rifles.

By ten-thirty the brass band of the invader was playing

beautiful and sentimental music in the town square while the townsmen, their mouths a little open and their eyes astonished, stood about listening to the music and staring at the gray-helmeted men who carried sub-machine guns in their arms.

By ten-thirty-eight the riddled six were buried, the parachutes were folded, and the battalion was billeted in Mr. Corell's warehouse by the pier, which had on its shelves blankets and cots for a battalion.

By ten-forty-five old Mayor Orden had received the formal request that he grant an audience to Colonel Lanser of the invaders, an audience which was set for eleven sharp at the Mayor's five-room palace.

The drawing-room of the palace was very sweet and comfortable. The gilded chairs covered with their worn tapestry were set about stiffly like too many servants with nothing to do. An arched marble fireplace held its little basket of red flameless heat, and a hand-painted coal scuttle stood on the hearth. On the mantel, flanked by fat vases, stood a large, curly porcelain clock which swarmed with tumbling cherubs. The wallpaper of the room was dark red with gold figures, and the woodwork was white, pretty, and clean. The paintings on the wall were largely preoccupied with the amazing heroism of large dogs faced with imperiled children. Nor water nor fire nor earthquake could do in a child so long as a big dog was available.

Beside the fireplace old Doctor Winter sat, bearded and simple and benign, historian and physician to the town. He watched in amazement while his thumbs rolled over and over on his lap. Doctor Winter was a man so simple that only a profound man would know him as profound. He looked up at Joseph, the Mayor's servingman, to see whether Joseph had observed the rolling wonders of his thumbs.

"Eleven o'clock?" Doctor Winter asked.

And Joseph answered abstractedly, "Yes, sir. The note said eleven."

"You read the note?"

"No, sir, His Excellency read the note to me."

And Joseph went about testing each of the gilded chairs to see whether it had moved since he had last placed it. Joseph habitually scowled at furniture, expecting it to be impertinent, mischievous, or dusty. In a world where Mayor Orden was the leader of men, Joseph was the leader of furniture, silver, and dishes. Joseph was elderly and lean and serious, and his life was so complicated that only a profound man would know him to be simple. He saw nothing amazing about Doctor Winter's rolling thumbs; in fact he found them irritating. Joseph suspected that something pretty important was happening, what with foreign soldiers in the town and the local army killed or captured. Sooner or later Joseph would have to get an opinion about it all. He wanted no levity, no rolling thumbs, no nonsense from furniture. Doctor Winter moved his chair a few inches from its appointed place and Joseph waited impatiently for the moment when he could put it back again.

Doctor Winter repeated, "Eleven o'clock, and they'll be here then, too. A time-minded people, Joseph."

And Joseph said, without listening, "Yes, sir."

"A time-minded people," the doctor repeated.

"Yes, sir," said Joseph.

"Time and machines."

"Yes, sir."

"They hurry toward their destiny as though it would not wait. They push the rolling world along with their shoulders."

And Joseph said, "Quite right, sir," simply because he was getting tired of saying, "Yes, sir."

Joseph did not approve of this line of conversation, since

it did not help him to have an opinion about anything. If Joseph remarked to the cook later in the day, "A time-minded people, Annie," it would not make any sense. Annie would ask, "Who?" and then "Why?" and finally say, "That's nonsense, Joseph." Joseph had tried carrying Doctor Winter's remarks below-stairs before and it had always ended the same: Annie always discovered them to be nonsense.

Doctor Winter looked up from his thumbs and watched Joseph disciplining the chairs. "What's the Mayor doing?"

"Dressing to receive the colonel, sir."

"And you aren't helping him? He will be ill dressed by himself."

"Madame is helping him. Madame wants him to look his best. She"—Joseph blushed a little—"Madame is trimming the hair out of his ears, sir. It tickles. He won't let me do it."

"Of course it tickles," said Doctor Winter.

"Madame insists," said Joseph.

Doctor Winter laughed suddenly. He stood up and held his hands to the fire and Joseph skillfully darted behind him and replaced the chair where it should be.

"We are so wonderful," the doctor said. "Our country is falling, our town is conquered, the Mayor is about to receive the conqueror, and Madame is holding the struggling Mayor by the neck and trimming the hair out of his ears."

"He was getting very shaggy," said Joseph. "His eyebrows, too. His Excellency is even more upset about having his eyebrows trimmed than his ears. He says it hurts. I doubt if even Madame can do it."

"She will try," Doctor Winter said.

"She wants him to look his best, sir."

Through the glass window of the entrance door a helmeted face looked in and there was a rapping on the door.

It seemed that some warm light went out of the room and
a little grayness took its place.

Doctor Winter looked up at the clock and said, "They
are early. Let them in, Joseph."

Joseph went to the door and opened it. A soldier stepped
in, dressed in a long coat. He was helmeted and he carried
a sub-machine gun over his arm. He glanced quickly about
and then stepped aside. Behind him an officer stood in the
doorway. The officer's uniform was common and it had
rank showing only on the shoulders.

The officer stepped inside and looked at Doctor Winter.
He was rather like an overdrawn picture of an English gentleman. He had a slouch, his face was red, his nose long but
rather pleasing; he seemed about as unhappy in his uniform
as most British general officers are. He stood in the doorway,
staring at Doctor Winter, and he said, "Are you Mayor Orden, sir?"

Doctor Winter smiled. "No, no, I am not."

"You are an official, then?"

"No, I am the town doctor and I am a friend of the
Mayor."

The officer said, "Where is Mayor Orden?"

"Dressing to receive you. You are the colonel?"

"No, I am not. I am Captain Bentick." He bowed and
Doctor Winter returned the bow slightly. Captain Bentick
continued, as though a little embarrassed at what he had to
say. "Our military regulations, sir, prescribe that we search
for weapons before the commanding officer enters a room.
We mean no disrespect, sir." And he called over his shoulder, "Sergeant!"

The sergeant moved quickly to Joseph, ran his hands over
his pockets, and said, "Nothing, sir."

Captain Bentick said to Doctor Winter, "I hope you will

pardon us." And the sergeant went to Doctor Winter and patted his pockets. His hands stopped at the inside coat pocket. He reached quickly in, brought out a little, flat, black leather case, and took it to Captain Bentick. Captain Bentick opened the case and found there a few simple surgical instruments—two scalpels, some surgical needles, some clamps, a hypodermic needle. He closed the case again and handed it back to Doctor Winter.

Doctor Winter said, "You see, I am a country doctor. One time I had to perform an appendectomy with a kitchen knife. I have always carried these with me since then."

Captain Bentick said, "I believe there are some firearms here?" He opened a little leather book that he carried in his pocket.

Doctor Winter said, "You are thorough."

"Yes, our local man has been working here for some time."

Doctor Winter said, "I don't suppose you would tell who that man is?"

Bentick said, "His work is all done now. I don't suppose there would be any harm in telling. His name is Corell."

And Doctor Winter said in astonishment, "George Corell? Why, that seems impossible! He's done a lot for this town. Why, he even gave prizes for the shooting-match in the hills this morning." And as he said it his eyes began to understand what had happened and his mouth closed slowly, and he said, "I see; that is why he gave the shooting-match. Yes, I see. But George Corell—that sounds impossible!"

The door to the left opened and Mayor Orden came in; he was digging in his right ear with his little finger. He was dressed in his official morning coat, with his chain of office about his neck. He had a large, white, spraying mustache and two smaller ones, one over each eye. His white hair was so recently brushed that only now were the hairs struggling to be free, to stand up again. He had been Mayor so long that he was the Idea-Mayor in the town. Even grown people when they saw the word "mayor," printed or written, saw Mayor Orden in their minds. He and his office were one. It had given him dignity and he had given it warmth.

From behind him Madame emerged, small and wrinkled and fierce. She considered that she had created this man out of whole cloth, had thought him up, and she was sure that she could do a better job if she had it to do again. Only once or twice in her life had she ever understood all of him, but the part of him which she knew, she knew intricately and well. No little appetite or pain, no carelessness or meanness in him escaped her; no thought or dream or longing in him ever reached her. And yet several times in her life she had seen the stars.

She stepped around the Mayor and she took his hand and pulled his finger out of his outraged ear and pushed his hand to his side, the way she would take a baby's thumb away from his mouth.

"I don't believe for a moment it hurts as much as you say," she said, and to Doctor Winter, "He won't let me fix his eyebrows."

"It hurts," said Mayor Orden.

"Very well, if you want to look like that there is nothing I can do about it." She straightened his already straight tie. "I'm glad you're here, Doctor," she said. "How many do you think will come?" And then she looked up and saw Captain Bentick. "Oh," she said, "the colonel!"

Captain Bentick said, "No, ma'am, I'm only preparing for the colonel. Sergeant!"

The sergeant, who had been turning over pillows, looking behind pictures, came quickly to Mayor Orden and ran his hands over his pockets.

Captain Bentick said, "Excuse him, sir, it's regulations."

He glanced again at the little book in his hand. "Your Excellency, I think you have firearms here. Two items, I believe?"

Mayor Orden said, "Firearms? Guns, you mean, I guess. Yes, I have a shotgun and a sporting-rifle." He said deprecatingly, "You know, I don't hunt very much any more. I always think I'm going to, and then the season opens and I don't get out. I don't take the pleasure in it I used to."

Captain Bentick insisted. "Where are these guns, Your Excellency?"

The Mayor rubbed his cheek and tried to think.. "Why, I think—" He turned to Madame. "Weren't they in the back of that cabinet in the bedroom with the walking-sticks?"

Madame said, "Yes, and every stitch of clothing in that cabinet smells of oil. I wish you'd put them somewhere else."

Captain Bentick said, "Sergeant!" and the sergeant went quickly into the bedroom.

"It's an unpleasant duty. I'm sorry," said the captain.

The sergeant came back, carrying a double-barreled shot-gun and a rather nice sporting-rifle with a shoulder strap. He leaned them against the side of the entrance door.

Captain Bentick said, "That's all, thank you, Your Excellency. Thank you, Madame."

He turned and bowed slightly to Doctor Winter. "Thank you, Doctor. Colonel Lanser will be here directly. Good morning!"

And he went out of the front door, followed by the sergeant with the two guns in one hand and the sub-machine gun over his right arm.

Madame said, "For a moment I thought he was the colonel. He was a rather nice-looking young man."

Doctor Winter said sardonically, "No, he was just protecting the colonel."

Madame was thinking, "I wonder how many officers will come?" And she looked at Joseph and saw that he was shamelessly eavesdropping. She shook her head at him and frowned and he went back to the little things he had been doing. He began dusting all over again.

And Madame said, "How many do you think will come?"

Doctor Winter pulled out a chair outrageously and sat down again. "I don't know," he said.

"Well"—she frowned at Joseph—"we've been talking it over. Should we offer them tea or a glass of wine? If we do, I don't know how many there will be, and if we don't, what are we to do?"

Doctor Winter shook his head and smiled. "I don't know. It's been so long since we conquered anybody or anybody conquered us. I don't know what is proper."

Mayor Orden had his finger back in his itching ear. He said, "Well, I don't think we should. I don't think the people would like it. I don't want to drink wine with them. I don't know why."

Madame appealed to the doctor then. "Didn't people in the old days—the leaders, that is—compliment each other and take a glass of wine?"

Doctor Winter nodded. "Yes, indeed they did." He shook his head slowly. "Maybe that was different. Kings and princes played at war the way Englishmen play at hunting. When the fox was dead they gathered at a hunt breakfast. But Mayor Orden is probably right: the people might not like him to drink wine with the invader."

Madame said, "The people are down listening to the music. Annie told me. If they can do that, why shouldn't we keep civilized procedure alive?"

The Mayor looked steadily at her for a moment and his voice was sharp. "Madame, I think with your permission we will not have wine. The people are confused now. They have lived at peace so long that they do not quite believe in war. They will learn and then they will not be confused any more. They elected me not to be confused. Six town boys were murdered this morning. I think we will have no hunt breakfast. The people do not fight wars for sport."

Madame bowed slightly. There had been a number of times in her life when her husband had become the Mayor. She had learned not to confuse the Mayor with her husband.

Mayor Orden looked at his watch and when Joseph came in, carrying a small cup of black coffee, he took it absent-mindedly. "Thank you," he said, and he sipped it. "I should be clear," he said apologetically to Doctor Winter. "I should be—do you know how many men the invader has?"

"Not many," the doctor said. "I don't think over two hundred and fifty; but all with those little machine guns."

The Mayor sipped his coffee again and made a new start. "What about the rest of the country?"

The doctor raised his shoulders and dropped them again.

"Was there no resistance anywhere?" the Mayor went on hopelessly.

And again the doctor raised his shoulders. "I don't know. The wires are cut or captured. There is no news."

"And our boys, our soldiers?"

"I don't know," said the doctor.

Joseph interrupted. "I heard—that is, Annie heard—"

"What, Joseph?"

"Six men were killed, sir, by the machine guns. Annie heard three were wounded and captured."

"But there were twelve."

"Annie heard that three escaped."

The Mayor turned sharply. "Which ones escaped?" he demanded.

"I don't know, sir. Annie didn't hear."

Madame inspected a table for dust with her finger. She said, "Joseph, when they come, stay close to your bell. We might want some little thing. And put on your other coat, Joseph, the one with the buttons." She thought for a moment. "And, Joseph, when you finish what you are told to do, go out of the room. It makes a bad impression when you just stand around listening. It's provincial, that's what it is."

"Yes, Madame," Joseph said.

"We won't serve wine, Joseph, but you might have some cigarettes handy in that little silver conserve box. And don't strike the match to light the colonel's cigarette on your shoe. Strike it on the match-box."

"Yes, Madame."

Mayor Orden unbuttoned his coat and took out his watch and looked at it and put it back and buttoned his coat again, one button too high. Madame went to him and rebuttoned it correctly.

Doctor Winter asked, "What time is it?"

"Five of eleven."

"A time-minded people," the doctor said. "They will be here on time. Do you want me to go away?"

Mayor Orden looked startled. "Go? No—no, stay." He laughed softly. "I'm a little afraid," he said apologetically. "Well, not afraid, but I'm nervous." And he said helplessly, "We have never been conquered, for a long time—" He stopped to listen. In the distance there was a sound of band music, a march. They all turned in its direction and listened.

Madame said, "Here they come. I hope not too many try to crowd in here at once. It isn't a very big room."

Doctor Winter said sardonically, "Madame would prefer the Hall of Mirrors at Versailles?"

She pinched her lips and looked about, already placing the conquerors with her mind. "It is a very small room," she said.

The band music swelled a little and then grew fainter. There came a gentle tap on the door.

"Now, who can that be? Joseph, if it is anyone, tell him to come back later. We are very busy."

The tap came again. Joseph went to the door and opened it a crack and then a little wider. A gray figure, helmeted and gantleted, appeared.

"Colonel Lanser's compliments," the head said. "Colonel Lanser requests an audience with Your Excellency."

Joseph opened the door wide. The helmeted orderly stepped inside and looked quickly about the room and then stood aside. "Colonel Lanser!" he announced.

A second helmeted figure walked into the room, and his rank showed only on his shoulders. Behind him came a rather short man in a black business suit. The colonel was a middle-aged man, gray and hard and tired-looking. He had the square shoulders of a soldier, but his eyes lacked the blank look of the ordinary soldier. The little man beside him was bald and rosy-cheeked, with small black eyes and a sensual mouth.

Colonel Lanser took off his helmet. With a quick bow, he said, "Your Excellency!" He bowed to Madame. "Madame!" And he said, "Close the door, please, Corporal." Joseph quickly shut the door and stared in small triumph at the soldier.

Lanser looked questioningly at the doctor, and Mayor Orden said, "This is Doctor Winter."

"An official?" the colonel asked.

"A doctor, sir, and, I might say, the local historian."

Lanser bowed slightly. He said, "Doctor Winter, I do not mean to be impertinent, but there will be a page in your history, perhaps—"

And Doctor Winter smiled. "Many pages, perhaps."

Colonel Lanser turned slightly toward his companion. "I think you know Mr. Corell," he said.

The Mayor said, "George Corell? Of course I know him. How are you, George?"

Doctor Winter cut in sharply. He said, very formally, "Your Excellency, our friend, George Corell, prepared this town for the invasion. Our benefactor, George Corell, sent our soldiers into the hills. Our dinner guest, George Corell, has made a list of every firearm in the town. Our friend, George Corell!"

Corell said angrily, "I work for what I believe in! That is an honorable thing."

Orden's mouth hung a little open. He was bewildered. He looked helplessly from Winter to Corell. "This isn't true," he said. "George, this isn't true! You have sat at my table, you have drunk port with me. Why, you helped me plan the hospital! This isn't true!"

He was looking very steadily at Corell and Corell looked belligerently back at him. There was a long silence. Then the Mayor's face grew slowly tight and very formal and his whole body was rigid. He turned to Colonel Lanser and he said, "I do not wish to speak in this gentleman's company."

Corell said, "I have a right to be here! I am a soldier like the rest. I simply do not wear a uniform."

The Mayor repeated, "I do not wish to speak in this gentleman's presence."

Colonel Lanser said, "Will you leave us now, Mr. Corell?"

And Corell said, "I have a right to be here!"

Lanser repeated sharply, "Will you leave us now, Mr. Corell? Do you outrank me?"

"Well, no, sir."

"Please go, Mr. Corell," said Colonel Lanser.

And Corell looked at the Mayor angrily, and then he turned and went quickly out of the doorway. Doctor Winter chuckled and said, "That's good enough for a paragraph in my history." Colonel Lanser glanced sharply at him but he did not speak.

Now the door on the right opened, and straw-haired red-eyed Annie put an angry face into the doorway. "There's soldiers on the back porch, Madame," she said. "Just standing there."

"They won't come in," Colonel Lanser said. "It's only military procedure."

Madame said icily, "Annie, if you have anything to say, let Joseph bring the message."

"I didn't know but they'd try to get in," Annie said. "They smelled the coffee."

"Annie!"

"Yes, Madame," and she withdrew.

The colonel said, "May I sit down?" And he explained, "We have been a long time without sleep."

The Mayor seemed to start out of sleep himself. "Yes," he said, "of course, sit down!"

The colonel looked at Madame and she seated herself and he settled tiredly into a chair. Mayor Orden stood, still half dreaming.

The colonel began, "We want to get along as well as we can. You see, sir, this is more like a business venture than anything else. We need the coal mine here and the fishing. We will try to get along with just as little friction as possible."

The Mayor said, "I have had no news. What about the rest of the country?"

"All taken," said the colonel. "It was well planned."

"Was there no resistance anywhere?"

The colonel looked at him compassionately. "I wish there had not been. Yes, there was some resistance, but it only caused bloodshed. We had planned very carefully."

Orden stuck to his point. "But there was resistance?"

"Yes, but it was foolish to resist. Just as here, it was destroyed instantly. It was sad and foolish to resist."

Doctor Winter caught some of the Mayor's anxiousness about the point. "Yes," he said, "foolish, but they resisted?"

And Colonel Lanser replied, "Only a few and they are gone. The people as a whole are quiet."

Doctor Winter said, "The people don't know yet what has happened."

"They are discovering," said Lanser. "They won't be foolish again." He cleared his throat and his voice became brisk. "Now, sir, I must get to business. I'm really very tired, but before I can sleep I must make my arrangements." He sat forward in his chair. "I am more engineer than soldier. This whole thing is more an engineering job than conquest. The coal must come out of the ground and be shipped. We have technicians, but the local people will continue to work the mine. Is that clear? We do not wish to be harsh."

And Orden said, "Yes, that's clear enough. But suppose the people do not want to work the mine?"

The colonel said, "I hope they will want to, because they must. We must have the coal."

"But if they don't?"

"They must. They are an orderly people. They don't want trouble." He waited for the Mayor's reply and none came. "Is that not so, sir?" the colonel asked.

Mayor Orden twisted his chain. "I don't know, sir. They

are orderly under their own government. I don't know how
they would be under yours. It is untouched ground, you
see. We have built our government over four hundred
years."

The colonel said quickly, "We know that, and so we are
going to keep your government. You will still be the Mayor,
you will give the orders, you will penalize and reward. In
that way, they will not give trouble."

Mayor Orden looked at Doctor Winter. "What are you
thinking about?"

"I don't know," said Doctor Winter. "It would be interesting to see. I'd expect trouble. This might be a bitter
people."

Mayor Orden said, "I don't know, either." He turned to
the colonel. "Sir, I am of this people, and yet I don't know
what they will do. Perhaps you know. Or maybe it would
be different from anything you know or we know. Some
people accept appointed leaders and obey them. But my
people have elected me. They made me and they can un-
make me. Perhaps they will if they think I have gone over
to you. I just don't know."

The colonel said, "You will be doing them a service if
you keep them in order."

"A service?"

"Yes, a service. It is your duty to protect them from
harm. They will be in danger if they are rebellious. We must
get the coal, you see. Our leaders do not tell us how; they
order us to get it. But you have your people to protect. You
must make them do the work and thus keep them safe."

Mayor Orden asked, "But suppose they don't want to be
safe?"

"Then you must think for them."

Orden said, a little proudly, "My people don't like to

have others think for them. Maybe they are different from your people. I am confused, but that I am sure of."

Now Joseph came in quickly and he stood leaning forward, bursting to speak. Madame said, "What is it, Joseph? Get the silver box of cigarettes."

"Pardon, Madame," said Joseph. "Pardon, Your Excellency."

"What do you want?" the Mayor asked.

"It's Annie," he said. "She's getting angry, sir."

"What is the matter?" Madame demanded.

"Annie doesn't like the soldiers on the back porch."

The colonel asked, "Are they causing trouble?"

"They are looking through the door at Annie," said Joseph. "She hates that."

The colonel said, "They are carrying out orders. They are doing no harm."

"Well, Annie hates to be stared at," said Joseph.

Madame said, "Joseph, tell Annie to take care."

"Yes, Madame," and Joseph went out.

The colonel's eyes dropped with tiredness. "There's another thing, Your Excellency," he said. "Would it be possible for me and my staff to stay here?"

Mayor Orden thought a moment and he said, "It's a small place. There are larger, more comfortable places."

Then Joseph came back with the silver box of cigarettes and he opened it and held it in front of the colonel. When the colonel took one, Joseph ostentatiously lighted it. The colonel puffed deeply.

"It isn't that," he said. "We have found that when a staff lives under the roof of the local authority, there is more tranquillity."

"You mean," said Orden, "the people feel there is collaboration involved?"

"Yes, I suppose that is it."

Mayor Orden looked hopelessly at Doctor Winter, and Winter could offer him nothing but a wry smile. Orden said softly, "Am I permitted to refuse this honor?"

"I'm sorry," the colonel said. "No. These are the orders of my leader."

"The people will not like it," Orden said.

"Always the people! The people are disarmed. The people have no say."

Mayor Orden shook his head. "You do not know, sir."

From the doorway came the sound of an angry woman's voice, and a thump and a man's cry. Joseph came scuttling through the door. "She's thrown boiling water," Joseph said. "She's very angry."

There were commands through the door and the clump of feet. Colonel Lanser got up heavily. "Have you no control over your servants, sir?" he asked.

Mayor Orden smiled. "Very little," he said. "She's a good cook when she is happy. Was anyone hurt?" he asked Joseph.

"The water was boiling, sir."

Colonel Lanser said, "We just want to do our job. It's an engineering job. You will have to discipline your cook."

"I can't," said Orden. "She'll quit."

"This is an emergency. She can't quit."

"Then she'll throw water," said Doctor Winter.

The door opened and a soldier stood in the opening. "Shall I arrest this woman, sir?"

"Was anyone hurt?" Lanser asked.

"Yes, sir, scalded, and one man bitten. We are holding her, sir."

Lanser looked helpless, then he said, "Release her and go outside and off the porch."

"Yes, sir," and the door closed behind the soldier.

Lanser said, "I could have her shot; I could lock her up."

"Then we would have no cook," said Orden.

"Look," said the colonel. "We are instructed to get along with your people."

Madame said, "Excuse me, sir, I will just go and see if the soldiers hurt Annie," and she went out.

Now Lanser stood up. "I told you I'm very tired, sir. I must have some sleep. Please co-operate with us for the good of all." When Mayor Orden made no reply, "For the good of all," Lanser repeated. "Will you?"

Orden said, "This is a little town. I don't know. The people are confused and so am I."

"But will you try to co-operate?"

Orden shook his head. "I don't know. When the town makes up its mind what it wants to do, I'll probably do that."

"But you are the authority."

Orden smiled. "You won't believe this, but it is true: authority is in the town. I don't know how or why, but it is so. This means we cannot act as quickly as you can, but when a direction is set, we all act together. I am confused. I don't know yet."

Lanser said wearily, "I hope we can get along together. It will be so much easier for everyone. I hope we can trust you. I don't like to think of the means the military will take to keep order."

Mayor Orden was silent.

"I hope we can trust you," Lanser repeated.

Orden put his finger in his ear and wiggled his hand. "I don't know," he said.

Madame came through the door then. "Annie is furious," she said. "She is next door, talking to Christine. Christine is angry, too."

"Christine is even a better cook than Annie," said the Mayor.

2

Upstairs in the little palace of the Mayor the staff of Colonel Lanser made its headquarters. There were five of them besides the colonel. There was Major Hunter, a haunted little man of figures, a little man who, being a dependable unit, considered all other men either as dependable units or as unfit to live. Major Hunter was an engineer, and except in case of war no one would have thought of giving him command of men. For Major Hunter set his men in rows like figures and he added and subtracted and multiplied them. He was an arithmetician rather than a mathematician. None of the humor, the music, or the mysticism of higher mathematics ever entered his head. Men might vary in height or weight or color, just as 6 is different from 8, but there was little other difference. He had been married several times and he did not know why his wives became very nervous before they left him.

Captain Bentick was a family man, a lover of dogs and pink children and Christmas. He was too old to be a captain, but a curious lack of ambition had kept him in that rank. Before the war he had admired the British country gentleman very much, wore English clothes, kept English dogs, smoked in an English pipe a special pipe mixture sent him from London, and subscribed to those country magazines which extol gardening and continually argue about the relative merits of English and Gordon setters. Captain Bentick spent all his holidays in Sussex and liked to be mistaken for an Englishman in Budapest or Paris. The war changed all that outwardly, but he had sucked on a pipe too long, had carried a stick too long, to give them up too suddenly. Once, five years before, he had written a letter to the *Times* about

grass dying in the Midlands and had signed it Edmund
Twitchell, Esq.; and, furthermore, the *Times* had printed it.

If Captain Bentick was too old to be a captain, Captain
Loft was too young. Captain Loft was as much a captain as
one can imagine. He lived and breathed his captaincy. He
had no unmilitary moments. A driving ambition forced him
up through the grades. He rose like cream to the top of
milk. He clicked his heels as perfectly as a dancer does. He
knew every kind of military courtesy and insisted on using
it all. Generals were afraid of him because he knew more
about the deportment of a soldier than they did. Captain
Loft thought and believed that a soldier is the highest de-
velopment of animal life. If he considered God at all, he
thought of Him as an old and honored general, retired and
gray, living among remembered battles and putting wreaths
on the graves of his lieutenants several times a year. Captain
Loft believed that all women fall in love with a uniform and
he did not see how it could be otherwise. In the normal
course of events he would be a brigadier-general at forty-
five and have his picture in the illustrated papers, flanked by
tall, pale, masculine women wearing lacy picture hats.

Lieutenants Prackle and Tonder were snot-noses, under-
graduates, lieutenants, trained in the politics of the day, be-
lieving the great new system invented by a genius so great
that they never bothered to verify its results. They were
sentimental young men, given to tears and to furies. Lieutenant Prackle carried a lock of hair in the back of his watch,
wrapped in a bit of blue satin, and the hair was constantly
getting loose and clogging the balance wheel, so that he
wore a wrist watch for telling time. Prackle was a dancing-
partner, a gay young man who nevertheless could scowl like
the Leader, could brood like the Leader. He hated degen-
erate art and had destroyed several canvases with his own
hands. In cabarets he sometimes made pencil sketches of his

companions which were so good that he had often been told
he should have been an artist. Prackle had several blond sisters of whom he was so proud that he had on occasion
caused a commotion when he thought they had been in-
sulted. The sisters were a little disturbed about it because
they were afraid someone might set out to prove the insults,
which would not have been hard to do. Lieutenant Prackle
spent nearly all his time off duty daydreaming of seducing
Lieutenant Tonder's blond sister, a buxom girl who loved
to be seduced by older men who did not muss her hair as
Lieutenant Prackle did.

Lieutenant Tonder was a poet, a bitter poet who dreamed
of perfect, ideal love of elevated young men for poor girls.
Tonder was a dark romantic with a vision as wide as his
experience. He sometimes spoke blank verse under his
breath to imaginary dark women. He longed for death on
the battlefield, with weeping parents in the background, and
the Leader, brave but sad in the presence of the dying youth.
He imagined his death very often, lighted by a fair setting
sun which glinted on broken military equipment, his men
standing silently around him, with heads sunk low, as over
a fat cloud galloped the Valkyries, big-breasted, mothers and
mistresses in one, while Wagnerian thunder crashed in the
background. And he even had his dying words ready.

These were the men of the staff, each one playing war as
children play "Run, Sheep, Run." Major Hunter thought
of war as an arithmetical job to be done so he could get
back to his fireplace; Captain Loft as the proper career of a
properly brought-up young man; and Lieutenants Prackle
and Tonder as a dreamlike thing in which nothing was very
real. And their war so far had been play—fine weapons and
fine planning against unarmed, planless enemies. They had
lost no fights and suffered little hurt. They were, under pres-
sure, capable of cowardice or courage, as everyone is. Of

them all, only Colonel Lanser knew what war really is in the long run.

Lanser had been in Belgium and France twenty years before and he tried not to think what he knew—that war is treachery and hatred, the muddling of incompetent generals, the torture and killing and sickness and tiredness, until at last it is over and nothing has changed except for new weariness and new hatreds. Lanser told himself he was a soldier, given orders to carry out. He was not expected to question or to think, but only to carry out orders; and he tried to put aside the sick memories of the other war and the certainty that this would be the same. This one will be different, he said to himself fifty times a day; this one will be very different.

In marching, in mobs, in football games, and in war, outlines become vague; real things become unreal and a fog creeps over the mind. Tension and excitement, weariness, movement—all merge in one great gray dream, so that when it is over, it is hard to remember how it was when you killed men or ordered them to be killed. Then other people who were not there tell you what it was like and you say vaguely, "Yes, I guess that's how it was."

This staff had taken three rooms on the upper floor of the Mayor's palace. In the bedrooms they had put their cots and blankets and equipment, and in the room next to them and directly over the little drawing-room on the ground floor they had made a kind of club, rather an uncomfortable club. There were a few chairs and a table. Here they wrote letters and read letters. They talked and ordered coffee and planned and rested. On the walls between the windows there were pictures of cows and lakes and little farmhouses, and from the windows they could look down over the town to the waterfront, to the docks where the shipping was tied up, to the docks where the coal barges pulled up and took their loads and went out to sea. They could look down over the little town that twisted past the square to the waterfront, and they could see the fishing-boats lying at anchor in the bay, the sails furled, and they could smell the drying fish on the beach, right through the window.

There was a large table in the center of the room and Major Hunter sat beside it. He had his drawing-board in his lap and resting on the table, and with a T-square and triangle he worked at a design for a new railroad siding. The drawing-board was unsteady and the major was growing angry with its unsteadiness. He called over his shoulder, "Prackle!" And then, "Lieutenant Prackle!"

The bedroom door opened and the lieutenant came out, half his face covered with shaving-cream. He held the brush in his hand. "Yes?" he said.

Major Hunter jiggled his drawing-board. "Hasn't that tripod for my board turned up in the baggage?"

"I don't know, sir," said Prackle. "I didn't look."

"Well, look now, will you? It's bad enough to have to work in this light. I'll have to draw this again before I ink it."

Prackle said, "Just as soon as I finish shaving, I'll look."

Hunter said irritably, "This siding is more important than your looks. See if there is a canvas case like a golf bag under that pile in there."

Prackle disappeared into the bedroom. The door to the right opened and Captain Loft came in. He wore his helmet, a pair of field glasses, sidearm, and various little leather cases strung all over him. He began to remove his equipment as soon as he entered.

"You know, that Bentick's crazy," he said. "He was going out on duty in a fatigue cap, right down the street."

Loft put his field glasses on the table and took off his helmet, then his gas-mask bag. A little pile of equipment began to heap up on the table.

Hunter said, "Don't leave that stuff there. I have to work here. Why shouldn't he wear a cap? There hasn't been any trouble. I get sick of these tin things. They're heavy and you can't see."

Loft said primly, "It's bad practice to leave it off. It's bad for the people here. We must maintain a military standard, an alertness, and never vary it. We'll just invite trouble if we don't."

"What makes you think so?" Hunter asked.

Loft drew himself up a little. His mouth thinned with certainty. Sooner or later everyone wanted to punch Loft in the nose for his sureness about things. He said, "I don't think it. I was paraphrasing *Manual X-12* on deportment in occupied countries. It is very carefully worked out." He began to say, "You—" and then changed it to, "Everybody should read *X-12* very closely."

Hunter said, "I wonder whether the man who wrote it was ever in occupied country. These people are harmless enough. They seem to be good, obedient people."

Prackle came through the door, his face still half covered with shaving-soap. He carried a brown canvas tube, and behind him came Lieutenant Tonder. "Is this it?" Prackle asked.

"Yes. Unpack it, will you, and set it up."

Prackle and Tonder went to work on the folding tripod and tested it and put it near Hunter. The major screwed his board to it, tilted it right and left, and finally settled gruntingly behind it.

Captain Loft said, "Do you know you have soap on your face, Lieutenant?"

"Yes, sir," Prackle said. "I was shaving when the major asked me to get the tripod."

"Well, you had better get it off," Loft said. "The colonel might see you."

"Oh, he wouldn't mind. He doesn't care about things like that."

Tonder was looking over Hunter's shoulder as he worked.

Loft said, "Well, he may not, but it doesn't look right."

Prackle took a handkerchief and rubbed the soap from his cheek. Tonder pointed to a little drawing on the corner of the major's board. "That's a nice-looking bridge, Major. But where in the world are we going to build a bridge?"

Hunter looked down at the drawing and then over his shoulder at Tonder. "Huh? Oh, that isn't any bridge we're going to build. Up here is the work drawing."

"What are you doing with a bridge, then?"

Hunter seemed a little embarrassed. "Well, you know, in my back yard at home I've got a model railroad line. I was going to bridge a little creek for it. Brought the line right down to the creek, but I never did get the bridge built. I thought I'd kind of work it out while I was away."

Lieutenant Prackle took from his pocket a folded roto-gravure page and he unfolded it and held it up and looked at it. It was a picture of a girl, all legs and dress and eyelashes, a well-developed blonde in black openwork stockings and a low bodice, and this particular blonde peeped over a black lace fan. Lieutenant Prackle held her up and he said, "Isn't she something?" Lieutenant Tonder looked critically at the picture and said, "I don't like her."

"What don't you like about her?"

"I just don't like her," said Tonder. "What do you want her picture for?"

Prackle said, "Because I do like her and I bet you do, too."

"I do not," said Tonder.

"You mean to say you wouldn't take a date with her if you could?" Prackle asked.

Tonder said, "No."

"Well, you're just crazy," and Prackle went to one of the curtains. He said, "I'm just going to stick her up here and let you brood about her for a while." He pinned the picture to the curtain.

Captain Loft was gathering his equipment into his arms now, and he said, "I don't think it looks very well out here, Lieutenant. You'd better take it down. It wouldn't make a good impression on the local people."

Hunter looked up from his board. "What wouldn't?" He followed their eyes to the picture. "Who's that?" he asked.

"She's an actress," said Prackle.

Hunter looked at her carefully. "Oh, do you know her?"

Tonder said, "She's a tramp."

Hunter said, "Oh, then you know her?"

Prackle was looking steadily at Tonder. He said, "Say, how do you know she's a tramp?"

"She looks like a tramp," said Tonder.

"Do you know her?"

"No, and I don't want to."

Prackle began to say, "Then how do you know?" when Loft broke in. He said, "You'd better take the picture down. Put it up over your bed if you want to. This room's kind of official here."

Prackle looked at him mutinously and was about to speak when Captain Loft said, "That's an order, Lieutenant," and poor Prackle folded his paper and put it into his pocket again. He tried cheerily to change the subject. "There are some pretty girls in this town, all right," he said. "As soon as we get settled down and everything going smoothly, I'm going to get acquainted with a few."

Loft said, "You'd better read X-12. There's a section dealing with sexual matters." And he went out, carrying his duffel, glasses, and equipment. Lieutenant Tonder, still look-

ing over Hunter's shoulder, said, "That's clever—the coal
cars come right through the mines to the ship."

Hunter came slowly out of his work and he said, "We
have to speed it up; we've got to get that coal moving. It's
a big job. I'm awful thankful that the people here are calm
and sensible."

Loft came back into the room without his equipment. He
stood by the window, looking out toward the harbor, toward the coal mine, and he said, "They are calm and sensible
because we are calm and sensible. I think we can take credit
for that. That's why I keep harping on procedure. It is very
carefully worked out."

The door opened and Colonel Lanser came in, removing
his coat as he entered. His staff gave him military courtesy
—not very rigid, but enough. Lanser said, "Captain Loft,
will you go down and relieve Bentick? He isn't feeling well,
says he's dizzy."

"Yes, sir," said Loft. "May I suggest, sir, that I only recently came off duty?"

Lanser inspected him closely. "I hope you don't mind
going, Captain."

"Not at all, sir; I just mention it for the record."

Lanser relaxed and chuckled. "You like to be mentioned
in the reports, don't you?"

"It does no harm, sir."

"And when you have enough mentions," Lanser went
on, "there will be a little dangler on your chest."

"They are the milestones in a military career, sir."

Lanser sighed. "Yes, I guess they are. But they won't be
the ones you'll remember, Captain."

"Sir?" Loft asked.

"You'll know what I mean later—perhaps."

Captain Loft put his equipment on rapidly. "Yes, sir," he
said, and went out and his footsteps clattered down the

wooden stairs, and Lanser watched him go with a little amusement. He said quietly, "There goes a born soldier." And Hunter looked up and poised his pencil and he said, "A born ass."

"No," said Lanser, "he's being a soldier the way a lot of men would be politicians. He'll be on the General Staff before long. He'll look down on war from above and so he'll always love it."

Lieutenant Prackle said, "When do you think the war will be over, sir?"

"Over? Over? What do you mean?"

Lieutenant Prackle continued, "How soon will we win?"

Lanser shook his head. "Oh, I don't know. The enemy is still in the world."

"But we will lick them," said Prackle.

Lanser said, "Yes?"

"Won't we?"

"Yes; yes, we always do."

Prackle said excitedly, "Well, if it's quiet around Christmas, do you think there will be some furloughs granted?"

"I don't know," said Lanser. "Such orders will have to come from home. Do you want to get home for Christmas?"

"Well, I'd kind of like to."

"Maybe you will," said Lanser, "maybe you will."

Lieutenant Tonder said, "We won't drop out of this occupation, will we, sir, after the war is over?"

"I don't know," said the Colonel. "Why?"

"Well," said Tonder, "it's a nice country, nice people. Our men—some of them—might even settle here."

Lanser said jokingly, "You've seen some place you like, perhaps?"

"Well," said Tonder, "there are some beautiful farms here. If four or five of them were thrown together, it would be a nice place to settle, I think."

"You have no family land, then?" Lanser asked.

"No, sir, not any more. Inflation took it away."

Lanser was tired now of talking to children. He said, "Ah, well, we still have a war to fight. We still have coal to take out. Do you suppose we can wait until it is over before we build up these estates? Such orders will come from above. Captain Loft can tell you that." His manner changed. He said, "Hunter, your steel will be in tomorrow. You can get your tracks started this week."

There was a knock at the door and a sentry put his head in. He said, "Mr. Corell wishes to see you, sir."

"Send him in," said the colonel. And he said to the others, "This is the man who did the preliminary work here. We might have some trouble with him."

"Did he do a good job?" Tonder asked.

"Yes, he did, and he won't be popular with the people here. I wonder whether he will be popular with us."

"He deserves credit, certainly," Tonder said.

"Yes," Lanser said, "and don't think he won't claim it."

Corell came in, rubbing his hands. He radiated good-will and good-fellowship. He was dressed still in his black business suit, but on his head there was a patch of white bandage, stuck to his hair with a cross of adhesive tape. He advanced to the center of the room and said, "Good morning, Colonel. I should have called yesterday after the trouble downstairs, but I knew how busy you would be."

The colonel said, "Good morning." Then with a circular gesture of his hand. "This is my staff, Mr. Corell."

"Fine boys," said Corell. "They did a good job. Well, I tried to prepare for them well."

Hunter looked down at his board and he took out an inking-pen and dipped it and began to ink in his drawing.

Lanser said, "You did very well. I wish you hadn't killed

those six men, though. I wish their soldiers hadn't come back."

Corell spread his hands and said comfortably, "Six men is a small loss for a town of this size, with a coal mine, too."

Lanser said sternly, "I am not averse to killing people if that finishes it. But sometimes it is better not to."

Corell had been studying the officers. He looked sideways at the lieutenants, and he said, "Could we—perhaps—talk alone, Colonel?"

"Yes, if you wish. Lieutenant Prackle and Lieutenant Tonder, will you go to your room, please?" And the colonel said to Corell, "Major Hunter is working. He doesn't hear anything when he's working." Hunter looked up from his board and smiled quietly and looked down again. The young lieutenants left the room, and when they were gone Lanser said, "Well, here we are. Won't you sit down?"

"Thank you, sir," and Corell sat down behind the table.

Lanser looked at the bandage on Corell's head. He said bluntly, "Have they tried to kill you already?"

Corell felt the bandage with his fingers. "This? Oh, this was a stone that fell from a cliff in the hills this morning."

"You're sure it wasn't thrown?"

"What do you mean?" Corell asked. "These aren't fierce people. They haven't had a war for a hundred years. They've forgotten about fighting."

"Well, you've lived among them," said the colonel. "You ought to know." He stepped close to Corell. "But if you are safe, these people are different from any in the world. I've helped to occupy countries before. I was in Belgium twenty years ago and in France." He shook his head a little as though to clear it, and he said gruffly, "You did a good job. We should thank you. I mentioned your work in my report."

"Thank you, sir," said Corell. "I did my best."

Lanser said, a little wearily, "Well, sir, now what shall we do? Would you like to go back to the capital? We can put you on a coal barge if you're in a hurry, or on a destroyer if you want to wait."

Corell said, "But I don't want to go back. I'll stay here."

Lanser studied this for a moment and he said, "You know, I haven't a great many men. I can't give you a very adequate bodyguard."

"But I don't need a bodyguard. I tell you these aren't violent people."

Lanser looked at the bandage for a moment. Hunter glanced up from his board and remarked, "You'd better start wearing a helmet." He looked down at his work again.

Now Corell moved forward in his chair. "I wanted particularly to talk to you, Colonel. I thought I might help with the civil administration."

Lanser turned on his heel and walked to the window and looked out, and then he swung around and said quietly, "What have you in mind?"

"Well, you must have a civil authority you can trust. I thought perhaps that Mayor Orden might step down now and—well, if I were to take over his office, it and the military would work very nicely together."

Lanser's eyes seemed to grow large and bright. He came close to Corell and he spoke sharply. "Have you mentioned this in your report?"

Corell said, "Well, yes, naturally—in my analysis."

Lanser interrupted. "Have you talked to any of the town people since we arrived—outside of the Mayor, that is?"

"Well, no. You see, they are still a bit startled. They didn't expect it." He chuckled. "No, sir, they certainly didn't expect it."

But Lanser pressed his point. "So you don't really know what's going on in their minds?"

"Why, they're startled," said Corell. "They're—well, they're almost dreaming."

"You don't know what they think of you?" Lanser asked.

"I have many friends here. I know everyone."

"Did anyone buy anything in your store this morning?"

"Well, of course, business is at a standstill," Corell answered. "No one's buying anything."

Lanser relaxed suddenly. He went to a chair and sat down and crossed his legs. He said quietly, "Yours is a difficult and brave branch of the service. It should be greatly rewarded."

"Thank you, sir."

"You will have their hatred in time," said the colonel.

"I can stand that, sir. They are the enemy."

Now Lanser hesitated a long moment before he spoke, and then he said softly, "You will not even have *our* respect."

Corell jumped to his feet excitedly. "This is contrary to the Leader's words!" he said. "The Leader has said that all branches are equally honorable."

Lanser went on very quietly, "I hope the Leader knows. I hope he can read the minds of soldiers." And then almost compassionately he said, "You should be greatly rewarded." For a moment he sat quietly and then he pulled himself together and said, "Now we must come to exactness. I am in charge here. My job is to get coal out. To do that I must maintain order and discipline, and to do that I must know what is in the minds of these people. I must anticipate revolt. Do you understand that?"

"Well, I can find out what you wish to know, sir. As Mayor here, I will be very effective," said Corell.

Lanser shook his head. "I have no orders about this. I must use my own judgment. I think you will never again know what is going on here. I think no one will speak to you; no one will be near to you except those people who will live on money, who can live on money. I think without a guard you will be in great danger. It will please me if you go back to the capital, there to be rewarded for your fine work."

"But my place is here, sir," said Corell. "I have made my place. It is all in my report."

Lanser went on as though he had not heard. "Mayor Orden is more than a mayor," he said. "He is his people. He knows what they are doing, thinking, without asking, because he will think what they think. By watching him I will know them. He must stay. That is my judgment."

Corell said, "My work, sir, merits better treatment than being sent away."

"Yes, it does," Lanser said slowly. "But to the larger work I think you are only a detriment now. If you are not hated yet, you will be. In any little revolt you will be the first to be killed. I think I will suggest that you go back."

Corell said stiffly, "You will, of course, permit me to wait for a reply to my report to the capital?"

"Yes, of course. But I shall recommend that you go back for your own safety. Frankly, Mr. Corell, you have no value here. But——well, there must be other plans and other countries. Perhaps you will go now to some new town in some new country. You will win new confidence in a new field. You may be given a larger town, even a city, a greater responsibility. I think I will recommend you highly for your work here."

Corell's eyes were shining with gratification. "Thank you, sir," he said. "I've worked hard. Perhaps you are right. But you must permit me to wait for the reply from the capital."

Lanser's voice was tight. His eyes were slitted. He said harshly, "Wear a helmet, keep indoors, do not go out at night, and, above all, do not drink. Trust no woman nor any man. Do you understand that?"

Corell looked pityingly at the colonel. "I don't think you understand. I have a little house. A pleasant country girl waits on me. I even think she's a little fond of me. These are simple, peaceful people. I know them."

Lanser said, "There are no peaceful people. When will you learn it? There are no friendly people. Can't you understand that? We have invaded this country—you, by what they call treachery, prepared for us." His face grew red and his voice rose. "Can't you understand that we are at war with these people?"

Corell said, a little smugly, "We have defeated them."

The colonel stood up and swung his arms helplessly, and Hunter looked up from his board and put his hand out to protect his board from being jiggled. Hunter said, "Careful now, sir. I'm inking in. I wouldn't want to do it all over again."

Lanser looked down at him and said, "Sorry," and went on as though he were instructing a class. He said, "Defeat is a momentary thing. A defeat doesn't last. We were defeated and now we attack. Defeat means nothing. Can't you understand that? Do you know what they are whispering behind doors?"

Corell asked, "Do you?"

"No, but I suspect."

Then Corell said insinuatingly, "Are you afraid, Colonel? Should the commander of this occupation be afraid?"

Lanser sat down heavily and said, "Maybe that's it." And he said disgustedly, "I'm tired of people who have not been at war who know all about it." He held his chin in his hand and said, "I remember a little old woman in Brussels—sweet face, white hair; she was only four feet eleven; delicate old hands. You could see the veins almost black against her skin. And her black shawl and her blue-white hair. She used to sing our national songs to us in a quivering, sweet voice. She always knew where to find a cigarette or a virgin." He dropped his hand from his chin, and he caught himself as though he had been asleep. "We didn't know her son had been executed," he said. "When we finally shot her, she had killed twelve men with a long, black hatpin. I have it yet at home. It has an enamel button with a bird over it, red and blue."

Corell said, "But you shot her?"

"Of course we shot her."

"And the murders stopped?" asked Corell.

"No, the murders did not stop. And when we finally retreated, the people cut off stragglers and they burned some and they gouged the eyes from some, and some they even crucified."

Corell said loudly, "These are not good things to say, Colonel."

"They are not good things to remember," said Lanser.

Corell said, "You should not be in command if you are afraid."

And Lanser answered softly, "I know how to fight, you see. If you know, at least you do not make silly errors."

"Do you talk this way to the young officers?"

Lanser shook his head. "No, they wouldn't believe me."

"Why do you tell me, then?"

"Because, Mr. Corell, your work is done. I remember one time—" and as he spoke there was a tumble of feet on the stairs and the door burst open. A sentry looked in and Captain Loft brushed past him. Loft was rigid and cold and military; he said, "There's trouble, sir."

"Trouble?"

"I have to report, sir, that Captain Bentick has been killed."

Lanser said, "Oh—yes—Bentick!"

There was the sound of a number of footsteps on the stairs and two stretcher-bearers came in, carrying a figure covered with blankets.

Lanser said, "Are you sure he's dead?"

"Quite sure," Loft said stiffly.

The lieutenants came in from the bedroom, their mouths a little open, and they looked frightened. Lanser said, "Put him down there," and he pointed to the wall beside the windows. When the bearers had gone, Lanser knelt and lifted a corner of the blanket and then quickly put it down again. And still kneeling, he looked at Loft and said, "Who did this?"

"A miner," said Loft.

"Why?"

"I was there, sir."

"Well, make your report, then! Make your report, damn it, man!"

Loft drew himself up and said formally, "I had just relieved Captain Bentick, as the colonel ordered. Captain Bentick was about to leave to come here when I had some trouble about a recalcitrant miner who wanted to quit work. He shouted something about being a free man. When I ordered him to work, he rushed at me with his pick. Captain Bentick tried to interfere." He gestured slightly toward the body.

Lanser, still kneeling, nodded slowly. "Bentick was a curious man," he said. "He loved the English. He loved everything about them. I don't think he liked to fight very much. . . . You captured the man?"

"Yes, sir," Loft said.

Lanser stood up slowly and spoke as though to himself.

"So it starts again. We will shoot this man and make twenty new enemies. It's the only thing we know, the only thing we know."

Prackle said, "What do you say, sir?"

Lanser answered, "Nothing, nothing at all. I was just thinking." He turned to Loft and said, "Please give my compliments to Mayor Orden and my request that he see me immediately. It is very important."

Major Hunter looked up, dried his inking-pen carefully, and put it away in a velvet-lined box.

3

In the town the people moved sullenly through the streets. Some of the light of astonishment was gone from their eyes, but still a light of anger had not taken its place. In the coal shaft the workingmen pushed the coal cars sullenly. The small tradesmen stood behind their counters and served the people, but no one communicated with them. The people spoke to one another in monosyllables, and everyone was thinking of the war, thinking of himself, thinking of the past and how it had suddenly been changed.

In the drawing-room of the palace of Mayor Orden a small fire burned and the lights were on, for it was a gray day outside and there was frost in the air. The room was itself undergoing a change. The tapestry-covered chairs were pushed back, the little tables out of the way, and through the doorway to the right Joseph and Annie were struggling to bring in a large square dining-table. They had it on its side. Joseph was in the drawing-room and Annie's red face showed through the door. Joseph maneuvered the legs around sideways, and he cried, "Don't push, Annie! Now!"

"I am 'now-ing,'" said Annie the red-nosed, the red-eyed, the angry. Annie was always a little angry and these soldiers, this occupation, did not improve her temper. Indeed, what for years had been considered simply a bad disposition was suddenly become a patriotic emotion. Annie had gained some little reputation as an exponent of liberty by throwing hot water on the soldiers. She would have thrown it on anyone who cluttered up her porch, but it just happened that she had become a heroine; and since anger had been the beginning of her success, Annie went on to

new successes by whipping herself into increased and constant anger.

"Don't scuff the bottom," Joseph said. The table wedged
in the doorway. "Steady!" Joseph warned.

"I am steady," said Annie.

Joseph stood off and studied the table, and Annie crossed
her arms and glared at him. He tested a leg. "Don't push,"
he said. "Don't push so hard." And by himself he got the
table through while Annie followed with crossed arms.
"Now, up she goes," said Joseph, and at last Annie helped
him settle it on four legs and move it to the center of the
room. "There," Annie said. "If His Excellency hadn't told
me to, I wouldn't have done it. What right have they got
moving tables around?"

"What right coming in at all?" said Joseph.

"None," said Annie.

"None," repeated Joseph. "I see it like they have no right
at all, but they do it, with their guns and their parachutes;
they do it, Annie."

"They got no right," said Annie. "What do they want
with a table in here, anyway? This isn't a dining-room."

Joseph moved a chair up to the table and he set it carefully
at the right distance from the table, and he adjusted it.
"They're going to hold a trial," he said. "They're going to
try Alexander Morden."

"Molly Morden's husband?"

"Molly Morden's husband."

"For bashing that fellow with a pick?"

"That's right," said Joseph.

"But he's a nice man," Annie said. "They've got no right
to try him. He gave Molly a big red dress for her birthday.
What right have they got to try Alex?"

"Well," Joseph explained, "he killed this fellow."

"Suppose he did; the fellow ordered Alex around. I heard

about it. Alex doesn't like to be ordered. Alex's been an alderman in his time, and his father, too. And Molly Morden makes a nice cake," Annie said charitably. "But her frosting gets too hard. What'll they do with Alex?"

"Shoot him," Joseph said gloomily.

"They can't do that."

"Bring up the chairs, Annie. Yes, they can. They'll just do it."

Annie shook a very rigid finger in his face. "You remember my words," she said angrily. "People aren't going to like it if they hurt Alex. People like Alex. Did he ever hurt anybody before? Answer me that!"

"No," said Joseph.

"Well, there, you see! If they hurt Alex, people are going to be mad and I'm going to be mad. I won't stand for it!"

"What will you do?" Joseph asked her.

"Why, I'll kill some of them myself," said Annie.

"And then they'll shoot you," said Joseph.

"Let them! I tell you, Joseph, things can go too far— tramping in and out all hours of the night, shooting people."

Joseph adjusted a chair at the head of the table, and he became in some curious way a conspirator. He said softly, "Annie."

She paused and, sensing his tone, walked nearer to him. He said, "Can you keep a secret?"

She looked at him with a little admiration, for he had never had a secret before. "Yes. What is it?"

"Well, William Deal and Walter Doggel got away last night."

"Got away? Where?"

"They got away to England, in a boat."

Annie sighed with pleasure and anticipation. "Does everybody know it?"

"Well, not everybody," said Joseph. "Everybody but—"
and he pointed a quick thumb toward the ceiling.

"When did they go? Why didn't I hear about it?"

"You were busy." Joseph's voice and face were cold.
"You know that Corell?"

"Yes."

Joseph came close to her. "I don't think he's going to
live long."

"What do you mean?" Annie asked.

"Well, people are talking."

Annie sighed with tension. "Ah-h-h!!"

Joseph at last had opinions. "People are getting together,"
he said. "They don't like to be conquered. Things are going
to happen. You keep your eyes peeled, Annie. There're going to be things for you to do."

Annie asked, "How about His Excellency? What's he going to do? How does His Excellency stand?"

"Nobody knows," said Joseph. "He doesn't say anything."

"He wouldn't be against us," Annie said.

"He doesn't say," said Joseph.

The knob turned on the left-hand door, and Mayor Or-
den came in slowly. He looked tired and old. Behind him
Doctor Winter walked. Orden said, "That's good, Joseph.
Thank you, Annie. It looks very well."

They went out and Joseph looked back through the door
for a moment before he closed it.

Mayor Orden walked to the fire and turned to warm his
back. Doctor Winter pulled out the chair at the head of the
table and sat down. "I wonder how much longer I can hold
this position?" Orden said. "The people don't quite trust me
and neither does the enemy. I wonder whether this is a good
thing."

"I don't know," said Winter. "You trust yourself, don't you? There's no doubt in your own mind?"

"Doubt? No. I am the Mayor. I don't understand many things." He pointed to the table.. "I don't know why they have to hold this trial in here. They're going to try Alex Morden here for murder. You remember Alex? He has that pretty little wife, Molly."

"I remember," said Winter. "She used to teach in the grammar school. Yes, I remember. She's so pretty, she hated to get glasses when she needed them. Well, I guess Alex killed an officer, all right. Nobody's questioned that."

Mayor Orden said bitterly, "Nobody questions it. But why do they try him? Why don't they shoot him? This is not a matter of doubt or certainty, justice or injustice. There's none of that here. Why must they try him—and in my house?"

Winter said, "I would guess it is for the show. There's an idea about it: if you go through the form of a thing, you have it, and sometimes people are satisfied with the form of a thing. We had an army—soldiers with guns—but it wasn't an army, you see. The invaders will have a trial and hope to convince the people that there is justice involved. Alex did kill the captain, you know."

"Yes, I see that," Orden said.

And Winter went on, "If it comes from your house, where the people expect justice—"

He was interrupted by the opening of the door to the right. A young woman entered. She was about thirty and quite pretty. She carried her glasses in her hand. She was dressed simply and neatly and she was very excited. She said quickly, "Annie told me to come right in, sir."

"Why, of course," said the Mayor. "You're Molly Morden."

"Yes, sir; I am. They say that Alex is to be tried and shot."

Orden looked down at the floor for a moment, and Molly went on, "They say you will sentence him. It will be your words that send him out."

Orden looked up, startled. "What's this? Who says this?"

"The people in the town." She held herself very straight and she asked, half pleadingly, half demandingly, "You wouldn't do that, would you, sir?"

"How could the people know what I don't know?" he said.

"That is a great mystery," said Doctor Winter. "That is a mystery that has disturbed rulers all over the world—how the people know. It disturbs the invaders now, I am told, how news runs through censorships, how the truth of things fights free of control. It is a great mystery."

The girl looked up, for the room had suddenly darkened, and she seemed to be afraid. "It's a cloud," she said. "There's word snow is on the way, and it's early, too." Doctor Winter went to the window and squinted up at the sky, and he said, "Yes, it's a big cloud; maybe it will pass over."

Mayor Orden switched on a lamp that made only a little circle of light. He switched it off again and said, "A light in the daytime is a lonely thing."

Now Molly came near to him again. "Alex is not a murdering man," she said. "He's a quick-tempered man, but he's never broken a law. He's a respected man."

Orden rested his hand on her shoulder and he said, "I have known Alex since he was a little boy. I knew his father and his grandfather. His grandfather was a bear-hunter in the old days. Did you know that?"

Molly ignored him. "You wouldn't sentence Alex?"

"No," he said. "How could I sentence him?"

"The people said you would, for the sake of order."

Mayor Orden stood behind a chair and gripped its back with his hands. "Do the people want order, Molly?"

"I don't know," she said. "They want to be free."

"Well, do they know how to go about it? Do they know what method to use against an armed enemy?"

"No," Molly said, "I don't think so."

"You are a bright girl, Molly; do you know?"

"No, sir, but I think the people feel that they are beaten if they are docile. They want to show these soldiers they're unbeaten."

"They've had no chance to fight. It's no fight to go against machine guns," Doctor Winter said.

Orden said, "When you know what they want to do, will you tell me, Molly?"

She looked at him suspiciously. "Yes—" she said.

"You mean 'no.' You don't trust me."

"But how about Alex?" she questioned.

"I'll not sentence him. He has committed no crime against our people," said the Mayor.

Molly was hesitant now. She said, "Will they—will they kill Alex?"

Orden stared at her and he said, "Dear child, my dear child."

She held herself rigid. "Thank you."

Orden came close to her and she said weakly, "Don't touch me. Please don't touch me. Please don't touch me." And his hand dropped. For a moment she stood still, then she turned stiffly and went out of the door.

She had just closed the door when Joseph entered. "Excuse me, sir, the colonel wants to see you. I said you were busy. I knew she was here. And Madame wants to see you, too."

Orden said, "Ask Madame to come in."

Joseph went out and Madame came in immediately.

"I don't know how I can run a house," she began; "it's more people than the house can stand. Annie's angry all the time."

"Hush!" Orden said.

Madame looked at him in amazement. "I don't know what—"

"Hush!" he said. "Sarah, I want you to go to Alex Morden's house. Do you understand? I want you to stay with Molly Morden while she needs you. Don't talk, just stay with her."

Madame said, "I've a hundred things—"

"Sarah, I want you to stay with Molly Morden. Don't leave her alone. Go now."

She comprehended slowly. "Yes," she said. "Yes, I will. When will it be over?"

"I don't know," he said. "I'll send Annie when it's time."

She kissed him lightly on the cheek and went out. Orden walked to the door and called, "Joseph, I'll see the colonel now."

Lanser came in. He had on a new pressed uniform with a little ornamental dagger at the belt. He said, "Good morning,, Your Excellency. I wish to speak to you informally." He glanced at Doctor Winter. "I should like to speak to you alone."

Winter went slowly to the door and as he reached it Orden said, "Doctor!"

Winter turned. "Yes?"

"Will you come back this evening?"

"You will have work for me?" the doctor asked.

"No—no. I just won't like to be alone."

"I will be here," said the doctor.

"And, Doctor, do you think Molly looked all right?"

"Oh, I think so. Close to hysteria, I guess. But she's good

stock. She's good, strong stock. She is a Kenderly, you know."

"I'd forgotten," Orden said. "Yes, she is a Kenderly, isn't she?"

Doctor Winter went out and shut the door gently behind him.

Lanser had waited courteously. He watched the door close. He looked at the table and the chairs about it. "I will not tell you, sir, how sorry I am about this. I wish it had not happened."

Mayor Orden bowed, and Lanser went on, "I like you, sir, and I respect you, but I have a job to do. You surely recognize that."

Orden did not answer. He looked straight into Lanser's eyes.

"We do not act alone or on our own judgment."

Between sentences Lanser waited for an answer but he received none.

"There are rules laid down for us, rules made in the capital. This man has killed an officer."

At last Orden answered, "Why didn't you shoot him then? That was the time to do it."

Lanser shook his head. "If I agreed with you, it would make no difference. You know as well as I that punishment is largely for the purpose of deterring the potential criminal. Thus, since punishment is for others than the punished, it must be publicized. It must even be dramatized." He thrust a finger in back of his belt and flipped his little dagger.

Orden turned away and looked out of the window at the dark sky. "It will snow tonight," he said.

"Mayor Orden, you know our orders are inexorable. We must get the coal. If your people are not orderly, we will have to restore that order by force." His voice grew stern.

"We must shoot people if it is necessary. If you wish to save your people from hurt, you must help us to keep order. Now, it is considered wise by my government that punishment emanate from the local authority. It makes for a more orderly situation."

Orden said softly, "So the people did know. That is a mystery." And louder he said, "You wish me to pass sentence of death on Alexander Morden after a trial here?"

"Yes, and you will prevent much bloodshed later if you will do it."

Orden went to the table and pulled out the big chair at its head and sat down. And suddenly he seemed to be the judge, with Lanser the culprit. He drummed with his fingers on the table. He said, "You and your government do not understand. In all the world yours is the only government and people with a record of defeat after defeat for centuries and every time because you did not understand people." He paused. "This principle does not work. First, I am the Mayor. I have no right to pass sentence of death. There is no one in this community with that right. If I should do it, I would be breaking the law as much as you."

"Breaking the law?" said Lanser.

"You killed six men when you came in. Under our law you are guilty of murder, all of you. Why do you go into this nonsense of law, Colonel? There is no law between you and us. This is war. Don't you know you will have to kill all of us or we in time will kill all of you? You destroyed the law when you came in, and a new law took its place. Don't you know that?"

Lanser said, "May I sit down?"

"Why do you ask? That is another lie. You could make me stand if you wished."

Lanser said, "No; it is true whether you believe it or not:

personally, I have respect for you and your office, and"—
he put his forehead in his hand for a moment—"you see,
what I think, sir, I, a man of a certain age and certain memories, is of no importance. I might agree with you, but that
would change nothing. The military, the political pattern I
work in has certain tendencies and practices which are in-
variable."

Orden said, "And these tendencies and practices have
been proven wrong in every single case since the beginning
of the world."

Lanser laughed bitterly. "I, an individual man with certain
memories, might agree with you, might even add that one
of the tendencies of the military mind and pattern is an inability to learn, an inability to see beyond the killing which
is its job. But I am not a man subject to memories. The coal
miner must be shot publicly, because the theory is that others
will then restrain themselves from killing our men."

Orden said, "We need not talk any more, then."

"Yes, we must talk. We want you to help."

Orden sat quietly for a while and then he said, "I'll tell
you what I'll do. How many men were on the machine
guns which killed our soldiers?"

"Oh, not more than twenty, I guess," said Lanser.

"Very well. If you will shoot them, I will condemn
Morden."

"You're not serious!" said the colonel.

"But I am serious."

"This can't be done. You know it."

"I know it," said Orden. "And what you ask cannot be
done."

Lanser said, "I suppose I knew. Corell will have to be
Mayor after all." He looked up quickly. "You will stay for
the trial?"

"Yes, I'll stay. Then Alex won't be so lonely."

Lanser looked at him and smiled a little sadly. "We have taken on a job, haven't we?"

"Yes," said the Mayor, "the one impossible job in the world, the one thing that can't be done."

"And that is?"

"To break man's spirit permanently."

Orden's head sank a little toward the table, and he said, without looking up, "It's started to snow. It didn't wait for night. I like the sweet, cool smell of the snow."

4

By eleven o'clock the snow was falling heavily in big, soft
puffs and the sky was not visible at all. People were scurrying
through the falling snow, and snow piled up in the doorways
and it piled up on the statue in the public square and on the
rails from the mine to the harbor. Snow piled up and the
little cartwheels skidded as they were pushed along. And
over the town there hung a blackness that was deeper than
the cloud, and over the town there hung a sullenness and a
dry, growing hatred. The people did not stand in the streets
long, but they entered the doors and the doors closed and
there seemed to be eyes looking from behind the curtains,
and when the military went through the street or when the
patrol walked down the main street, the eyes were on the
patrol, cold and sullen. And in the shops people came to buy
little things for lunch and they asked for the goods and got
it and paid for it and exchanged no good-day with the seller.

In the little palace drawing-room the lights were on and
the lights shone on the falling snow outside the window.
The court was in session. Lanser sat at the head of the table
with Hunter on his right, then Tonder, and, at the lower
end, Captain Loft with a little pile of papers in front of him.
On the opposite side, Mayor Orden sat on the colonel's left
and Prackle was next to him—Prackle, who scribbled on his
pad of paper. Beside the table two guards stood with bay-
onets fixed, with helmets on their heads, and they were little
wooden images. Between them was Alex Morden, a big
young man with a wide, low forehead, with deep-set eyes
and a long, sharp nose. His chin was firm and his mouth
sensual and wide. He was wide of shoulder, narrow of hip,
and in front of him his manacled hands clasped and un-

clasped. He was dressed in black trousers, a blue shirt open at the neck, and a dark coat shiny from wear.

Captain Loft read from the paper in front of him. " 'When ordered back to work, he refused to go, and when the order was repeated, the prisoner attacked Captain Loft with the pick-ax he carried. Captain Bentick interposed his body—' "

Mayor Orden coughed and, when Loft stopped reading, said, "Sit down, Alex. One of you guards get him a chair." The guard turned and pulled up a chair unquestioningly.

Loft said, "It is customary for the prisoner to stand."

"Let him sit down," Orden said. "Only we will know. You can report that he stood."

"It is not customary to falsify reports," said Loft.

"Sit down, Alex," Orden repeated.

And the big young man sat down and his manacled hands were restless in his lap.

Loft began, "This is contrary to all—"

The colonel said, "Let him be seated."

Captain Loft cleared his throat. " 'Captain Bentick interposed his body and received a blow on the head which crushed his skull.' A medical report is appended. Do you wish me to read it?"

"No need," said Lanser. "Make it as quick as you can."

" 'These facts have been witnessed by several of our soldiers, whose statements are attached. This military court finds that the prisoner is guilty of murder and recommends a death sentence.' Do you wish me to read the statements of the soldiers?"

Lanser sighed. "No." He turned to Alex. "You don't deny that you killed the captain, do you?"

Alex smiled sadly. "I hit him," he said. "I don't know that I killed him."

Orden said, "Good work, Alex!" And the two looked at each other as friends.

Loft said, "Do you mean to imply that he was killed by someone else?"

"I don't know," said Alex. "I only hit him, and then somebody hit me."

Colonel Lanser said, "Do you want to offer any explanation? I can't think of anything that will change the sentence, but we will listen."

Loft said, "I respectfully submit that the colonel should not have said that. It indicates that the court is not impartial."

Orden laughed dryly. The colonel looked at him and smiled a little. "Have you any explanation?" he repeated.

Alex lifted a hand to gesture and the other came with it. He looked embarrassed and put them in his lap again. "I was mad," he said. "I have a pretty bad temper. He said I must work. I am a free man. I got mad and I hit him. I guess I hit him hard. It was the wrong man." He pointed at Loft. "That's the man I wanted to hit, that one."

Lanser said, "It doesn't matter whom you wanted to hit. Anybody would have been the same. Are you sorry you did it?" He said aside to the table, "It would look well in the record if he were sorry."

"Sorry?" Alex asked. "I'm not sorry. He told me to go to work—me, a free man! I used to be alderman. He said I had to work."

"But if the sentence is death, won't you be sorry then?"

Alex sank his head and really tried to think honestly. "No," he said. "You mean, would I do it again?"

"That's what I mean."

"No," Alex said thoughtfully, "I don't think I'm sorry."

Lanser said, "Put in the record that the prisoner was over-

come with remorse. Sentence is automatic. Do you understand?" he said to Alex. "The court has no leeway. The
court finds you guilty and sentences you to be shot immediately. I do not see any reason to torture you with this any
more. Captain Loft, is there anything I have forgotten?"

"You've forgotten me," said Orden. He stood up and
pushed back his chair and stepped over to Alex. And Alex,
from long habit, stood up respectfully. "Alexander, I am the
elected Mayor."

"I know it, sir."

"Alex, these men are invaders. They have taken our
country by surprise and treachery and force."

Captain Loft said, "Sir, this should not be permitted."

Lanser said, "Hush! Is it better to hear it, or would you
rather it were whispered?"

Orden went on as though he had not been interrupted.
"When they came, the people were confused and I was confused. We did not know what to do or think. Yours was
the first clear act. Your private anger was the beginning of
a public anger. I know it is said in town that I am acting
with these men. I can show the town, but you—you are
going to die. I want you to know."

Alex dropped his head and then raised it. "I know, sir."

Lanser said, "Is the squad ready?"

"Outside, sir."

"Who is commanding?"

"Lieutenant Tonder, sir."

Tonder raised his head and his chin was hard and he held
his breath.

Orden said softly, "Are you afraid, Alex?"

And Alex said, "Yes, sir."

"I can't tell you not to be. I would be, too, and so would
these young—gods of war."

Lanser said, "Call your squad." Tonder got up quickly

and went to the door. "They're here, sir." He opened the door wide and the helmeted men could be seen.

Orden said, "Alex, go, knowing that these men will have no rest, no rest at all until they are gone, or dead. You will make the people one. It's a sad knowledge and little enough gift to you, but it is so. No rest at all."

Alex shut his eyes tightly. Mayor Orden leaned close and kissed him on the cheek. "Good-by, Alex," he said.

The guard took Alex by the arm and the young man kept his eyes tightly closed, and they guided him through the door. The squad faced about, and their feet marched away down out of the house and into the snow, and the snow muffled their footsteps.

The men about the table were silent. Orden looked toward the window and saw a little round spot being rubbed clear of snow by a quick hand. He stared at it, fascinated, and then he looked quickly away. He said to the colonel, "I hope you know what you are doing."

Captain Loft gathered his papers and Lanser asked, "In the square, Captain?"

"Yes, in the square. It must be public," Loft said.

And Orden said, "I hope you know."

"Man," said the colonel, "whether we know or not, it is what must be done."

Silence fell on the room and each man listened. And it was not long. From the distance there came a crash of firing. Lanser sighed deeply. Orden put his hand to his forehead and filled his lungs deeply. Then there was a shout outside. The glass of the window crashed inward and Lieutenant Prackle wheeled about. He brought his hand up to his shoulder and stared at it.

Lanser leaped up, crying, "So, it starts! Are you badly hurt, Lieutenant?"

"My shoulder," said Prackle.

Lanser took command. "Captain Loft, there will be tracks in the snow. Now, I want every house searched for firearms. I want every man who has one taken hostage. You, sir," he said to the Mayor, "are placed in protective custody. And understand this, please: we will shoot, five, ten, a hundred for one."

Orden said quietly, "A man of certain memories."

Lanser stopped in the middle of an order. He looked over slowly at the Mayor and for a moment they understood each other. And then Lanser straightened his shoulders. "A man of no memories!" he said sharply. And then, "I want every weapon in town gathered. Bring in everyone who resists. Hurry, before their tracks are filled."

The staff found their helmets and loosed their pistols and started out. And Orden went to the broken window. He said sadly, "The sweet, cool smell of the snow."

5

The days and the weeks dragged on, and the months dragged on. The snow fell and melted and fell and melted and finally fell and stuck. The dark buildings of the little town wore bells and hats and eyebrows of white and there were trenches through the snow to the doorways. In the harbor the coal barges came empty and went away loaded, but the coal did not come out of the ground easily. The good miners made mistakes. They were clumsy and slow. Machinery broke and took a long time to fix. The people of the conquered country settled in a slow, silent, waiting revenge. The men who had been traitors, who had helped the invaders—and many of them believed it was for a better state and an ideal way of life—found that the control they took was insecure, that the people they had known looked at them coldly and never spoke.

And there was death in the air, hovering and waiting. Accidents happened on the railroad, which clung to the mountains and connected the little town with the rest of the nation. Avalanches poured down on the tracks and rails were spread. No train could move unless the tracks were first inspected. People were shot in reprisal and it made no difference. Now and then a group of young men escaped and went to England. And the English bombed the coal mine and did some damage and killed some of both their friends and their enemies. And it did no good. The cold hatred grew with the winter, the silent, sullen hatred, the waiting hatred. The food supply was controlled—issued to the obedient and withheld from the disobedient—so that the whole population turned coldly obedient. There was a point where food could not be withheld, for a starving man cannot mine coal, cannot lift and carry. And the hatred was deep in the eyes of the people, beneath the surface.

Now it was that the conqueror was surrounded, the men of the battalion alone among silent enemies, and no man might relax his guard for even a moment. If he did, he disappeared, and some snowdrift received his body. If he went alone to a woman, he disappeared and some snowdrift received his body. If he drank, he disappeared. The men of the battalion could sing only together, could dance only together, and dancing gradually stopped and the singing expressed a longing for home. Their talk was of friends and relatives who loved them and their longings were for warmth and love, because a man can be a soldier for only so many hours a day and for only so many months in a year, and then he wants to be a man again, wants girls and drinks and music and laughter and ease, and when these are cut off, they become irresistibly desirable.

And the men thought always of home. The men of the battalion came to detest the place they had conquered, and they were curt with the people and the people were curt with them, and gradually a little fear began to grow in the conquerors, a fear that it would never be over, that they could never relax or go home, a fear that one day they would crack and be hunted through the mountains like rabbits, for the conquered never relaxed their hatred. The patrols, seeing lights, hearing laughter, would be drawn as to a fire, and when they came near, the laughter stopped, the warmth went out, and the people were cold and obedient. And the soldiers, smelling warm food from the little restaurants, went in and ordered the warm food and found that it was oversalted and overpeppered.

Then the soldiers read the news from home and from the other conquered countries, and the news was always good, and for a little while they believed it, and then after a while they did not believe it any more. And every man carried in his heart the terror. "If home crumbled, they would not tell us, and then it would be too late. These people will not spare us. They will kill us all." They remembered stories of their men retreating through Belgium and retreating out of Russia. And the more literate remembered the frantic, tragic retreat from Moscow, when every peasant's pitchfork tasted blood and the snow was rotten with bodies.

And they knew when they cracked, or relaxed, or slept too long, it would be the same here, and their sleep was restless and their days were nervous. They asked questions their officers could not answer because they did not know. They were not told, either. They did not believe the reports from home, either.

Thus it came about that the conquerors grew afraid of the conquered and their nerves wore thin and they shot at shadows in the night. The cold, sullen silence was with them always. Then three soldiers went insane in a week and cried all night and all day until they were sent away home. And others might have gone insane if they had not heard that mercy deaths awaited the insane at home, and a mercy death is a terrible thing to think of. Fear crept in on the men in their billets and it made them sad, and it crept into the patrols and it made them cruel.

The year turned and the nights grew long. It was dark at three o'clock in the afternoon and not light again until nine in the morning. The jolly lights did not shine out on the snow, for by law every window must be black against the bombers. And yet when the English bombers came over, some light always appeared near the coal mine. Sometimes the sentries shot a man with a lantern and once a girl with a flashlight. And it did no good. Nothing was cured by the shooting.

And the officers were a reflection of their men, more

restrained because their training was more complete, more resourceful because they had more responsibility, but the same fears were a little deeper buried in them, the same longings were more tightly locked in their hearts. And they were under a double strain, for the conquered people watched them for mistakes and their own men watched them for weakness, so that their spirits were taut to the breaking-point. The conquerors were under a terrible spiritual siege and everyone knew, conquered and conquerors, what would happen when the first crack appeared.

From the upstairs room of the Mayor's palace the comfort seemed to have gone. Over the windows black paper was tacked tightly and there were little piles of precious equipment about the room—the instruments and equipment that could not be jeopardized, the glasses and masks and helmets. And discipline here at least was laxer, as though these officers knew there must be some laxness somewhere or the machine would break. On the table were two gasoline lanterns which threw a hard, brilliant light and they made great shadows on the walls, and their hissing was an undercurrent in the room.

Major Hunter went on with his work. His drawing-board was permanently ready now, for the bombs tore out his work nearly as fast as he put it in. And he had little sorrow, for to Major Hunter building was life and here he had more building than he could project or accomplish. He sat at his drawing-board with a light behind him and his T-square moved up and down the board and his pencil was busy.

Lieutenant Prackle, his arm still in a sling, sat in a straight chair behind the center table, reading an illustrated paper. At the end of the table Lieutenant Tonder was writing a letter. He held his pen pinched high and occasionally he looked up from his letter and gazed at the ceiling, to find words to put in his letter.

Prackle turned a page of the illustrated paper and he said, "I can close my eyes and see every shop on this street here." And Hunter went on with his work and Tonder wrote a few more words. Prackle continued, "There is a restaurant right behind here. You can't see it in the picture. It's called Burden's."

Hunter did not look up. He said, "I know the place. They had good scallops."

"Sure they did," Prackle said. "Everything was good there. Not a single bad thing did they serve. And their coffee—"

Tonder looked up from his letter and said, "They won't be serving coffee now—or scallops."

"Well, I don't know about that," said Prackle. "They did and they will again. And there was a waitress there." He described her figure with his hand, with the good hand. "Blonde, so and so." He looked down at the magazine. "She had the strangest eyes—has, I mean—always kind of moist-looking as though she had just been laughing or crying." He glanced at the ceiling and he spoke softly. "I was out with her. She was lovely. I wonder why I didn't go back oftener. I wonder if she's still there."

Tonder said gloomily, "Probably not. Working in a factory, maybe."

Prackle laughed. "I hope they aren't rationing girls at home."

"Why not?" said Tonder.

Prackle said playfully, "You don't care much for girls, do you? Not much, you don't!"

Tonder said, "I like them for what girls are for. I don't let them crawl around my other life."

And Prackle said tauntingly, "It seems to me that they crawl all over you all the time."

Tonder tried to change the subject. He said, "I hate these damn lanterns. Major, when are you going to get that dynamo fixed?"

Major Hunter looked up slowly from his board and said, "It should be done by now. I've got good men working on it. I'll double the guard on it from now on, I guess."

"Did you get the fellow that wrecked it?" Prackle asked.

And Hunter said grimly, "It might be any one of five men. I got all five." He went on musingly, "It's so easy to wreck a dynamo if you know how. Just short it and it wrecks itself." He said, "The light ought to be on any time now."

Prackle still looked at his magazine. "I wonder when we will be relieved. I wonder when we will go home for a while. Major, wouldn't you like to go home for a rest?"

Hunter looked up from his work and his face was hopeless for a moment. "Yes, of course." He recovered himself. "I've built this siding four times. I don't know why a bomb always knocks out this particular siding. I'm getting tired of this piece of track. I have to change the route every time because of the craters. There's no time to fill them in. The ground is frozen too hard. It seems to be too much work."

Suddenly the electric lights came on and Tonder automatically reached out and turned off the two gasoline lanterns. The hissing was gone from the room.

Tonder said, "Thank God for that! That hissing gets on my nerves. It makes me think there's whispering." He folded the letter he had been writing and he said, "It's strange more letters don't come through. I've only had one in two weeks."

Prackle said, "Maybe nobody writes to you."

"Maybe," said Tonder. He turned to the major. "If anything happened—at home, I mean—do you think they would let us know—anything bad, I mean, any deaths or anything like that?"

Hunter said, "I don't know."

"Well," Tonder went on, "I would like to get out of this god-forsaken hole!"

Prackle broke in, "I thought you were going to live here after the war?" And he imitated Tonder's voice. "Put four or five farms together. Make a nice place, a kind of family seat. Wasn't that it? Going to be a little lord of the valley, weren't you? Nice, pleasant people, beautiful lawns and deer and little children. Isn't that the way it was, Tonder?"

As Prackle spoke, Tonder's hand dropped. Then he clasped his temples with his hands and he spoke with emotion. "Be still! Don't talk like that! These people! These horrible people! These cold people! They never look at you." He shivered. "They never speak. They answer like dead men. They obey, these horrible people. And the girls are frozen!"

There was a light tap on the door and Joseph came in with a scuttle of coal. He moved silently through the room and set the scuttle down so softly that he made no noise, and he turned without looking up at anyone and went toward the door again. Prackle said loudly, "Joseph!" And Joseph turned without replying, without looking up, and he bowed very slightly. And Prackle said still loudly, "Joseph, is there any wine or any brandy?" Joseph shook his head.

Tonder started up from the table, his face wild with anger, and he shouted, "Answer, you swine! Answer in words!"

Joseph did not look up. He spoke tonelessly. "No, sir; no, sir, there is no wine."

And Tonder said furiously, "And no brandy?"

Joseph looked down and spoke tonelessly again. "There is no brandy, sir." He stood perfectly still.

"What do you want?" Tonder said.

"I want to go, sir."

"Then go, goddamn it!"

Joseph turned and went silently out of the room and Tonder took a handkerchief out of his pocket and wiped his face. Hunter looked up at him and said, "You shouldn't let him beat you so easily."

Tonder sat down in his chair and put his hands to his temples and he said brokenly, "I want a girl. I want to go home. I want a girl. There's a girl in this town, a pretty girl. I see her all the time. She has blond hair. She lives beside the old-iron store. I want that girl."

Prackle said, "Watch yourself. Watch your nerves."

At that moment the lights went out again and the room was in darkness. Hunter spoke while the matches were being struck and an attempt was being made to light the lanterns; he said, "I thought I had all of them. I must have missed one. But I can't be running down there all the time. I've got good men down there."

Tonder lighted the first lantern and then he lighted the other, and Hunter spoke sternly to Tonder. "Lieutenant, do your talking to us if you have to talk. Don't let the enemy hear you talk this way. There's nothing these people would like better than to know your nerves are getting thin. Don't let the enemy hear you."

Tonder sat down again. The light was sharp on his face and the hissing filled the room. He said, "That's it! The enemy's everywhere! Every man, every woman, even children! The enemy's everywhere! Their faces look out of doorways. The white faces behind the curtains, listening. We have beaten them, we have won everywhere, and they wait and obey, and they wait. Half the world is ours. Is it the same in other places, Major?"

And Hunter said, "I don't know."

"That's it," Tonder said. "We don't know. The reports —everything in hand. Conquered countries cheer our soldiers, cheer the new order." His voice changed and grew soft and still softer. "What do the reports say about us? Do they say we are cheered, loved, flowers in our paths? Oh, these horrible people waiting in the snow!"

And Hunter said, "Now that's off your chest, do you feel better?"

Prackle had been beating the table softly with his good fist, and he said, "He shouldn't talk that way. He should keep things to himself. He's a soldier, isn't he? Then let him be a soldier."

The door opened quietly and Captain Loft came in and there was snow on his helmet and snow on his shoulders. His nose was pinched and red and his overcoat collar was high about his ears. He took off his helmet and the snow fell to the floor and he brushed his shoulders. "What a job!" he said.

"More trouble?" Hunter asked.

"Always trouble. I see they've got your dynamo again. Well, I think I fixed the mine for a while."

"What's your trouble?" Hunter asked.

"Oh, the usual thing with me—the slow-down and a wrecked dump car. I saw the wrecker, though. I shot him. I think I have a cure for it, Major, now. I just thought it up. I'll make each man take out a certain amount of coal. I can't starve the men or they can't work, but I've really got the answer. If the coal doesn't come out, no food for the families. We'll have the men eat at the mine, so there's no dividing at home. That ought to cure it. They work or their kids don't eat. I told them just now."

"What did they say?"

Loft's eyes narrowed fiercely. "Say? What do they ever say? Nothing! Nothing at all! But we'll see whether the coal comes out now." He took off his coat and shook it, and his eyes fell on the entrance door and he saw that it was open a crack. He moved silently to the door, jerked it open, then closed it. "I thought I had closed that door tight," he said.

"You did," said Hunter.

Prackle still turned the pages of his illustrated paper. His voice was normal again. "Those are monster guns we're using in the east. I never saw one of them. Did you, Captain?"

"Oh, yes," said Captain Loft. "I've seen them fired. They're wonderful. Nothing can stand up against them."

Tonder said, "Captain, do you get much news from home?"

"A certain amount," said Loft.

"Is everything well there?"

"Wonderful!" said Loft. "The armies move ahead everywhere."

"The British aren't defeated yet?"

"They are defeated in every engagement."

"But they fight on?"

"A few air raids, no more."

"And the Russians?"

"It's all over."

Tonder said insistently, "But they fight on?"

"A little skirmishing, no more."

"Then we have just about won, haven't we, Captain?" Tonder asked.

"Yes, we have."

Tonder looked closely at him and said, "You believe this, don't you, Captain?"

Prackle broke in, "Don't let him start that again!"

Loft scowled at Tonder. "I don't know what you mean."

Tonder said, "I mean this: we'll be going home before long, won't we?"

"Well, the reorganization will take some time," Hunter said. "The new order can't be put into effect in a day, can it?"

Tonder said, "All our lives, perhaps?"

And Prackle said, "Don't let him start it again!"

Loft came very close to Tonder and he said, "Lieutenant, I don't like the tone of your questions. I don't like the tone of doubt."

Hunter looked up and said, "Don't be hard on him, Loft. He's tired. We're all tired."

"Well, I'm tired, too," said Loft, "but I don't let treasonable doubts get in."

Hunter said, "Don't bedevil him, I tell you! Where's the colonel, do you know?"

"He's making out his report. He's asking for reinforcements," said Loft. "It's a bigger job than we thought."

Prackle asked excitedly, "Will he get them—the reinforcements?"

"How would I know?"

Tonder smiled. "Reinforcements!" he said softly. "Or maybe replacements. Maybe we could go home for a while." And he said, smiling, "Maybe I could walk down the street and people would say, 'Hello,' and they'd say, 'There goes a soldier,' and they'd be glad for me and they'd be glad of me. And there'd be friends about, and I could turn my back to a man without being afraid."

Prackle said, "Don't start that again! Don't let him get out of hand again!"

And Loft said disgustedly, "We have enough trouble now without having the staff go crazy."

But Tonder went on, "You really think replacements will come, Captain?"

"I didn't say so."

"But you said they might."

"I said I didn't know. Look, Lieutenant, we've conquered half the world. We must police it for a while. You know that."

"But the other half?" Tonder asked.

"They will fight on hopelessly for a while," said Loft.

"Then we must be spread out all over."

"For a while," said Loft.

Prackle said nervously, "I wish you'd make him shut up. I wish you would shut him up. Make him stop it."

Tonder got out his handkerchief and blew his nose, and he spoke a little like a man out of his head. He laughed embarrassedly. He said, "I had a funny dream. I guess it was a dream. Maybe it was a thought. Maybe a thought or a dream."

Prackle said, "Make him stop, Captain!"

Tonder said, "Captain, is this place conquered?"

"Of course," said Loft.

A little note of hysteria crept into Tonder's laughter. He said, "Conquered and we're afraid; conquered and we're surrounded." His laughter grew shrill. "I had a dream—or a thought—out in the snow with the black shadows and the faces in the doorways, the cold faces behind curtains. I had a thought or a dream."

Prackle said, "Make him stop!"

Tonder said, "I dreamed the Leader was crazy."

And Loft and Hunter laughed together and Loft said, "The enemy have found out how crazy. I'll have to write that one home. The papers would print that one. The enemy have learned how crazy the Leader is."

And Tonder went on laughing. "Conquest after conquest, deeper and deeper into molasses." His laughter choked him and he coughed into his handkerchief. "Maybe the Leader is crazy. Flies conquer the flypaper. Flies capture two hundred miles of new flypaper!" His laughter was growing more hysterical now.

Prackle leaned over and shook him with his good hand, "Stop it! You stop it! You have no right!"

And gradually Loft recognized that the laughter was hysterical and he stepped close to Tonder and slapped him in the face. He said, "Lieutenant, stop it!"

Tonder's laughter went on and Loft slapped him again in the face and he said, "Stop it, Lieutenant! Do you hear me?"

Suddenly Tonder's laughter stopped and the room was quiet except for the hissing of the lanterns. Tonder looked in amazement at his hand and he felt his bruised face with his hand and he looked at his hand again and his head sank down toward the table. "I want to go home," he said.

6

There was a little street not far from the town square where small peaked roofs and little shops were mixed up together. The snow was beaten down on the walks and in the street, but it piled high on the fences and it puffed on the roof peaks. It drifted against the shuttered windows of the little houses. And into the yards paths were shoveled. The night was dark and cold and no light showed from the windows to attract the bombers. And no one walked in the streets, for the curfew was strict. The houses were dark lumps against the snow. Every little while the patrol of six men walked down the street, peering about, and each man carried a long flashlight. The hushed tramp of their feet sounded in the street, the squeaks of their boots on the packed snow. They were muffled figures deep in thick coats; under their helmets were knitted caps which came down over their ears and covered their chins and mouths. A little snow fell, only a little, like rice.

The patrol talked as they walked, and they talked of things that they longed for—of meat and of hot soup and of the richness of butter, of the prettiness of girls and of their smiles and of their lips and their eyes. They talked of these things and sometimes they talked of their hatred of what they were doing and of their loneliness.

A small, peak-roofed house beside the iron shop was shaped like the others and wore its snow cap like the others. No light came from its shuttered windows and its storm doors were tightly closed. But inside a lamp burned in the small living-room and the door to the bedroom was open and the door to the kitchen was open. An iron stove was against the back wall with a little coal fire burning in it. It was a warm, poor, comfortable room, the floor covered with worn carpet, the walls papered in warm brown with an old-fashioned fleur-de-lis figure in gold. And on the back wall were two pictures, one of fish lying dead on a plate of ferns and the other of grouse lying dead on a fir bough. On the right wall there was a picture of Christ walking on the waves toward the despairing fishermen. Two straight chairs were in the room and a couch covered with a bright blanket. There was a little round table in the middle of the room, on which stood a kerosene lamp with a round flowered shade on it, and the light in the room was warm and soft.

The inner door, which led to the passage, which in turn led to the storm door, was beside the stove.

In a cushioned old rocking-chair beside the table Molly Morden sat alone. She was unraveling the wool from an old blue sweater and winding the yarn on a ball. She had quite a large ball of it. And on the table beside her was her knitting with the needles sticking in it, and a large pair of scissors. Her glasses lay on the table beside her, for she did not need them for knitting. She was pretty and young and neat. Her golden hair was done up on the top of her head and a blue bow was in her hair. Her hands worked quickly with the raveling. As she worked, she glanced now and then at the door to the passage. The wind whistled in the chimney softly, but it was a quiet night, muffled with snow.

Suddenly she stopped her work. Her hands were still. She looked toward the door and listened. The tramping feet of the patrol went by in the street and the sound of their voices could be heard faintly. The sound faded away. Molly ripped out new yarn and wound it on the ball. And again she stopped. There was a rustle at the door and then three short knocks. Molly put down her work and went to the door.

"Yes?" she called.

She unlocked the door and opened it and a heavily

cloaked figure came in. It was Annie, the cook, red-eyed and wrapped in mufflers. She slipped in quickly, as though practiced at getting speedily through doors and getting them closed again behind her. She stood there red-nosed, sniffling and glancing quickly around the room.

Molly said, "Good evening, Annie. I didn't expect you tonight. Take your things off and get warm. It's cold out."

Annie said, "The soldiers brought winter early. My father always said a war brought bad weather, or bad weather brought a war. I don't remember which."

"Take off your things and come to the stove."

"I can't," said Annie importantly. "They're coming."

"Who are coming?" Molly said.

"His Excellency," said Annie, "and the doctor and the two Anders boys."

"Here?" Molly asked. "What for?"

Annie held out her hand and there was a little package in it. "Take it," she said. "I stole it from the colonel's plate. It's meat."

And Molly unwrapped the little cake of meat and put it in her mouth and she spoke around her chewing. "Did you get some?"

Annie said, "I cook it, don't I? I always get some."

"When are they coming?"

Annie sniffled. "The Anders boys are sailing for England. They've got to. They're hiding now."

"Are they?" Molly asked. "What for?"

"Well, it was their brother, Jack, was shot today for wrecking that little car. The soldiers are looking for the rest of the family. You know how they do."

"Yes," Molly said, "I know how they do. Sit down, Annie."

"No time," said Annie. "I've got to get back and tell His Excellency it's all right here."

Molly said, "Did anybody see you come?"

Annie smiled proudly. "No, I'm awful good at sneaking."

"How will the Mayor get out?"

Annie laughed. "Joseph is going to be in his bed in case they look in, right in his nightshirt, right next to Madame!" And she laughed again. She said, "Joseph better lie pretty quiet."

Molly said, "It's an awful night to be sailing."

"It's better than being shot."

"Yes, so it is. Why is the Mayor coming here?"

"I don't know. He wants to talk to the Anders boys. I've got to go now, but I came to tell you."

Molly said, "How soon are they coming?"

"Oh, maybe half, maybe three-quarters of an hour," Annie said. "I'll come in first. Nobody bothers with old cooks." She started for the door and she turned midway, and as though accusing Molly of saying the last words she said truculently, "I'm not so old!" And she slipped out of the door and closed it behind her.

Molly went on knitting for a moment and then she got up and went to the stove and lifted the lid. The glow of the fire lighted her face. She stirred the fire and added a few lumps of coal and closed the stove again. Before she could get to her chair, there was a knocking on the outer door. She crossed the room and said to herself, "I wonder what she forgot." She went into the passage and she said, "What do you want?"

A man's voice answered her. She opened the door and a man's voice said, "I don't mean any harm. I don't mean any harm."

Molly backed into the room and Lieutenant Tonder followed her in. Molly said, "Who are you? What do you want? You can't come in here. What do you want?"

Lieutenant Tonder was dressed in his great gray overcoat.

He entered the room and took off his helmet and he spoke pleadingly. "I don't mean any harm. Please let me come in."

Molly said, "What do you want?"

She shut the door behind him and he said, "Miss, I only want to talk, that's all. I want to hear you talk. That's all I want."

"Are you forcing yourself on me?" Molly asked.

"No, miss, just let me stay a little while and then I'll go."

"What is it you want?"

Tonder tried to explain. "Can you understand this—can you believe this? Just for a little while, can't we forget this war? Just for a little while. Just for a little while, can't we talk together like people—together?"

Molly looked at him for a long time and then a smile came to her lips. "You don't know who I am, do you?"

Tonder said, "I've seen you in the town I know you're lovely. I know I want to talk to you."

And Molly still smiled. She said softly, "You don't know who I am." She sat in her chair and Tonder stood like a child, looking very clumsy. Molly continued, speaking quietly, "Why, you're lonely. It's as simple as that, isn't it?"

Tonder licked his lips and he spoke eagerly. "That's it," he said. "You understand. I knew you would. I knew you'd have to." His words came tumbling out. "I'm lonely to the point of illness. I'm lonely in the quiet and the hatred." And he said pleadingly, "Can't we talk, just a little bit?"

Molly picked up her knitting. She looked quickly at the front door. "You can stay not more than fifteen minutes. Sit down a little, Lieutenant."

She looked at the door again. The house creaked. Tonder became tense and he said, "Is someone here?"

"No, the snow is heavy on the roof. I have no man any more to push it down."

Tonder said gently, "Who did it? Was it something we did?"

And Molly nodded, looking far off. "Yes."

He sat down. "I'm sorry." After a moment he said, "I wish I could do something. I'll have the snow pushed off the roof."

"No," said Molly, "no."

"Why not?"

"Because the people would think I had joined with you. They would expel me. I don't want to be expelled."

Tonder said, "Yes, I see how that would be. You all hate us. But I'll take care of you if you'll let me."

Now Molly knew she was in control, and her eyes narrowed a little cruelly and she said, "Why do you ask? You are the conqueror. Your men don't have to ask. They take what they want."

"That's not what I want," Tonder said. "That's not the way I want it."

And Molly laughed, still a little cruelly. "You want me to like you, don't you, Lieutenant?"

He said simply, "Yes," and he raised his head and he said, "You are so beautiful, so warm. Your hair is bright. Oh, I've seen no kindness in a woman's face for so long!"

"Do you see any in mine?" she asked.

He looked closely at her. "I want to."

She dropped her eyes at last. "You're making love to me, aren't you, Lieutenant?"

And he said clumsily, "I want you to like me. Surely I want you to like me. Surely I want to see that in your eyes. I have seen you in the streets. I have watched you pass by. I've given orders that you mustn't be molested. Have you been molested?"

And Molly said quietly, "Thank you; no, I've not been molested."

His words rushed on. "Why, I've even written a poem for you. Would you like to see my poem?"

And she said sardonically, "Is it a long poem? You have to go very soon."

He said, "No, it's a little tiny poem. It's a little bit of a poem." He reached inside his tunic and brought out a folded paper and handed it to her. She leaned close to the lamp and put on her glasses and she read quietly.

> *Your eyes in their deep heavens*
> *Possess me and will not depart;*
> *A sea of blue thoughts rushing*
> *And pouring over my heart.*

She folded the paper and put it in her lap. "Did you write this, Lieutenant?"

"Yes."

She said a little tauntingly, "To me?"

And Tonder answered uneasily, "Yes."

She looked at him steadily, smiling. "You didn't write it, Lieutenant, did you?"

He smiled back like a child caught in a lie. "No."

Molly asked him, "Do you know who did?"

Tonder said, "Yes, Heine wrote it. It's '*Mit deinen blauen Augen.*' I've always loved it." He laughed embarrassedly and Molly laughed with him, and suddenly they were laughing together. He stopped laughing just as suddenly and a bleakness came into his eyes. "I haven't laughed like that since forever." He said, "They told us the people would like us, would admire us. They do not. They only hate us." And then he changed the subject as though he worked against time. "You are so beautiful. You are as beautiful as the laughter."

Molly said, "You're beginning to make love to me, Lieutenant. You must go in a moment."

And Tonder said, "Maybe I want to make love to you. A man needs love. A man dies without love. His insides shrivel and his chest feels like a dry chip. I'm lonely."

Molly got up from her chair. She looked nervously at the door and she walked to the stove and, coming back, her face grew hard and her eyes grew punishing and she said, "Do you want to go to bed with me, Lieutenant?"

"I didn't say that! Why do you talk that way?"

Molly said cruelly, "Maybe I'm trying to disgust you. I was married once. My husband is dead. You see, I'm not a virgin." Her voice was bitter.

Tonder said, "I only want you to like me."

And Molly said, "I know. You are a civilized man. You know that love-making is more full and whole and delightful if there is liking, too."

Tonder said, "Don't talk that way! Please don't talk that way!"

Molly glanced quickly at the door. She said, "We are a conquered people, Lieutenant. You have taken the food away. I'm hungry. I'll like you better if you feed me."

Tonder said, "What are you saying?"

"Do I disgust you, Lieutenant? Maybe I'm trying to. My price is two sausages."

Tonder said, "You can't talk this way!"

"What about your own girls, Lieutenant, after the last war? A man could choose among your girls for an egg or a slice of bread. Do you want me for nothing, Lieutenant? Is the price too high?"

He said, "You fooled me for a moment. But you hate me, too, don't you? I thought maybe you wouldn't."

"No, I don't hate you," she said, "I'm hungry and—I hate you!"

Tonder said, "I'll give you anything you need, but—"

And she interrupted him. "You want to call it something else? You don't want a whore. Is that what you mean?"

Tonder said, "I don't know what I mean. You make it sound full of hatred."

Molly laughed. She said, "It's not nice to be hungry. Two sausages, two fine, fat sausages can be the most precious things in the world."

"Don't say those things," he said. "Please don't!"

"Why not? They're true."

"They aren't true! This can't be true!"

She looked at him for a moment and then she sat down and her eyes fell to her lap and she said, "No, it's not true. I don't hate you. I'm lonely, too. And the snow is heavy on the roof."

Tonder got up and moved near to her. He took one of her hands in both of his and he said softly, "Please don't hate me. I'm only a lieutenant. I didn't ask to come here. You didn't ask to be my enemy. I'm only a man, not a conquering man."

Molly's fingers encircled his hand for a moment and she said softly, "I know; yes, I know."

And Tonder said, "We have some little right to life in all this death."

She put her hand to his cheek for a moment and she said, "Yes."

"I'll take care of you," he said. "We have some right to life in all the killing." His hand rested on her shoulder. Suddenly she grew rigid and her eyes were wide and staring as though she saw a vision. His hand released her and he asked, "What's the matter? What is it?" Her eyes stared straight ahead and he repeated, "What is it?"

Molly spoke in a haunted voice. "I dressed him like a little boy for his first day in school. And he was afraid. I buttoned his shirt and tried to comfort him, but he was beyond comfort. And he was afraid."

Tonder said, "What are you saying?"

And Molly seemed to see what she described. "I don't know why they let him come home. He was confused. He didn't know what was happening. He didn't even kiss me when he went away. He was afraid, and very brave, like a little boy on his first day of school."

Tonder stood up. "That was your husband."

Molly said, "Yes, my husband. I went to the Mayor, but he was helpless. And then he marched away—not very well nor steadily—and you took him out and you shot him. It was more strange than terrible then. I didn't quite believe it then."

Tonder said, "Your husband!"

"Yes; and now in the quiet house, I believe it. Now with the heavy snow on the roof, I believe it. And in the loneliness before daybreak, in the half-warmed bed, I know it then."

Tonder stood in front of her. His face was full of misery. "Good night," he said. "God keep you. May I come back?"

And Molly looked at the wall and at the memory. "I don't know," she said.

"I'll come back."

"I don't know."

He looked at her and then he quietly went out of the door, and Molly still stared at the wall. "God keep me!" She stayed for a moment staring at the wall. The door opened silently and Annie came in. Molly did not even see her.

Annie said disapprovingly, "The door was open."

Molly looked slowly toward her, her eyes still wide open. "Yes. Oh, yes, Annie."

"The door was open. There was a man came out. I saw him. He looked like a soldier."

And Molly said, "Yes, Annie."

"Was it a soldier here?"

"Yes, it was a soldier."

And Annie asked suspiciously, "What was he doing here?"

"He came to make love to me."

Annie said, "Miss, what are you doing? You haven't joined them, have you? You aren't with them, like that Corell?"

"No, I'm not with them, Annie."

Annie said, "If the Mayor's here and they come back, it'll be your fault if anything happens; it'll be your fault!"

"He won't come back. I won't let him come back."

But the suspicion stayed with Annie. She said, "Shall I tell them to come in now? Do you say it's safe?"

"Yes, it's safe. Where are they?"

"They're out behind the fence," said Annie.

"Tell them to come in."

And while Annie went out, Molly got up and smoothed her hair and she shook her head, trying to be alive again. There was a little sound in the passage. Two tall, blond young men entered. They were dressed in pea-jackets and dark turtle-neck sweaters. They wore stocking caps perched on their heads. They were wind-burned and strong and they looked almost like twins, Will Anders and Tom Anders, the fishermen.

"Good evening, Molly. You've heard?"

"Annie told me. It's a bad night to go."

Tom said, "It's better than a clear night. The planes see you on a clear night. What's the Mayor want, Molly?"

"I don't know. I heard about your brother. I'm sorry."

The two were silent and they looked embarrassed. Tom said, "You know how it is, better than most."

"Yes; yes, I know."

Annie came in the door again and she said in a hoarse whisper, "They're here!" And Mayor Orden and Doctor Winter came in. They took off their coats and caps and laid them on the couch. Orden went to Molly and kissed her on the forehead.

"Good evening, dear."

He turned to Annie. "Stand in the passage, Annie. Give us one knock for the patrol, one when it's gone, and two for danger. You can leave the outer door open a crack so you can hear if anyone comes."

Annie said, "Yes, sir." She went into the passage and shut the door behind her.

Doctor Winter was at the stove, warming his hands. "We got word you boys were going tonight."

"We've got to go," Tom said.

Orden nodded. "Yes, I know. We heard you were going to take Mr. Corell with you."

Tom laughed bitterly. "We thought it would be only right. We're taking his boat. We can't leave him around. It isn't good to see him in the streets."

Orden said sadly, "I wish he had gone away. It's just a danger to you, taking him."

"It isn't good to see him in the streets," Will echoed his brother. "It isn't good for the people to see him here."

Winter asked, "Can you take him? Isn't he cautious at all?"

"Oh, yes, he's cautious, in a way. At twelve o'clock, though, he walks to his house usually. We'll be behind the wall. I think we can get him through his lower garden to the water. His boat's tied up there. We were on her today getting her ready."

Orden repeated, "I wish you didn't have to. It's just an added danger. If he makes a noise, the patrol might come."

Tom said, "He won't make a noise, and it's better if he

disappears at sea. Some of the town people might get him and then there would be too much killing. No, it's better if he goes to sea."

Molly took up her knitting again. She said, "Will you throw him overboard?"

Will blushed. "He'll go to sea, ma'am." He turned to the Mayor. "You wanted to see us, sir?"

"Why, yes, I want to talk to you. Doctor Winter and I have tried to think—there's so much talk about justice, injustice, conquest. Our people are invaded, but I don't think they're conquered."

There was a sharp knock on the door and the room was silent. Molly's needles stopped, and the Mayor's outstretched hand remained in the air. Tom, scratching his ear, left his hand there and stopped scratching. Everyone in the room was motionless. Every eye was turned toward the door. Then, first faintly and then growing louder, there came the tramp of the patrol, the squeak of their boots in the snow, and the sound of their talking as they went by. They passed the door and their footsteps disappeared in the distance. There was a second tap on the door. And in the room the people relaxed.

Orden said, "It must be cold out there for Annie." He took up his coat from the couch and opened the inner door and handed his coat through. "Put this around your shoulders, Annie," he said and closed the door.

"I don't know what I'd do without her," he said. "She gets everywhere, she sees and hears everything."

Tom said, "We should be going pretty soon, sir."

And Winter said, "I wish you'd forget about Mr. Corell."

"We can't. It isn't good to see him in the streets." He looked inquiringly at Mayor Orden.

Orden began slowly. "I want to speak simply. This is a little town. Justice and injustice are in terms of little things.

Your brother's shot and Alex Morden's shot. Revenge against a traitor. The people are angry and they have no way to fight back. But it's all in little terms. It's people against people, not idea against idea."

Winter said, "It's funny for a doctor to think of destruction, but I think all invaded people want to resist. We are disarmed; our spirits and bodies aren't enough. The spirit of a disarmed man sinks."

Will Anders asked, "What's all this for, sir? What do you want of us?"

"We want to fight them and we can't," Orden said. "They're using hunger on the people now. Hunger brings weakness. You boys are sailing for England. Maybe nobody will listen to you, but tell them from us—from a small town—to give us weapons."

Tom asked, "You want guns?"

Again there was a quick knock on the door and the people froze where they were, and from outside there came the sound of the patrol, but at double step, running. Will moved quickly toward the door. The running steps came abreast of the house. There were muffled orders and the patrol ran by, and there was a second tap at the door.

Molly said, "They must be after somebody. I wonder who this time."

"We should be going," Tom said uneasily. "Do you want guns, sir? Shall we ask for guns?"

"No, tell them how it is. We are watched. Any move we make calls for reprisal. If we could have simple, secret weapons, weapons of stealth, explosives, dynamite to blow up rails, grenades, if possible, even poison." He spoke angrily. "This is no honorable war. This is a war of treachery and murder. Let us use the methods that have been used on us! Let the British bombers drop their big bombs on the works, but let them also drop us little bombs to use, to hide, to slip under the rails, under tanks. Then we will be armed, secretly armed. Then the invader will never know which of us is armed. Let the bombers bring us simple weapons. We will know how to use them!"

Winter broke in. "They'll never know where it will strike. The soldiers, the patrol, will never know which of us is armed."

Tom wiped his forehead. "If we get through, we'll tell them, sir, but—well, I've heard it said that in England there are still men in power who do not dare to put weapons in the hands of common people."

Orden stared at him. "Oh! I hadn't thought of that. Well, we can only see. If such people still govern England and America, the world is lost, anyway. Tell them what we say, if they will listen. We must have help, but if we get it"—his face grew very hard—"if we get it, we will help ourselves."

Winter said, "If they will even give us dynamite to hide, to bury in the ground to be ready against need, then the invader can never rest again, never! We will blow up his supplies."

The room grew excited. Molly said fiercely, "Yes, we could fight his rest, then. We could fight his sleep. We could fight his nerves and his certainties."

Will asked quietly, "Is that all, sir?"

"Yes." Orden nodded. "That's the core of it."

"What if they won't listen?"

"You can only try, as you are trying the sea tonight."

"Is that all, sir?"

The door opened and Annie came quietly in. Orden went on, "That's all. If you have to go now, let me send Annie out to see that the way is clear." He looked up and saw that Annie had come in. Annie said, "There's a soldier coming

up the path. He looks like the soldier that was here before.
There was a soldier here with Molly before."

The others looked at Molly. Annie said, "I locked the
door."

"What does he want?" Molly asked. "Why does he come
back?"

There was a gentle knocking at the outside door. Orden
went to Molly. "What is this, Molly? Are you in trouble?"

"No," she said, "no! Go out the back way. You can get
out through the back. Hurry, hurry out!"

The knocking continued on the front door. A man's
voice called softly. Molly opened the door to the kitchen.
She said, "Hurry, hurry!"

The Mayor stood in front of her. "Are you in trouble,
Molly? You haven't done anything?"

Annie said coldly, "It looks like the same soldier. There
was a soldier here before."

"Yes," Molly said to the Mayor. "Yes, there was a soldier
here before."

The Mayor said, "What did he want?"

"He wanted to make love to me."

"But he didn't?" Orden said.

"No," she said, "he didn't. Go now, and I'll take care."
Orden said, "Molly, if you're in trouble, let us help you."

"The trouble I'm in no one can help me with," she said.
"Go now," and she pushed them out of the door.

Annie remained behind. She looked at Molly. "Miss,
what does this soldier want?"

"I don't know what he wants."

"Are you going to tell him anything?"

"No." Wonderingly, Molly repeated, "No." And then
sharply she said, "No, Annie, I'm not!"

Annie scowled at her. "Miss, you'd better not tell him

anything!" And she went out and closed the door behind her.

The tapping continued on the front door and a man's
voice could be heard through the door.

Molly went to the center lamp, and her burden was heavy
on her. She looked down at the lamp. She looked at the
table, and she saw the big scissors lying beside her knitting.
She picked them up wonderingly by the blades. The blades
slipped through her fingers until she held the long shears and
she was holding them like a knife, and her eyes were hor-
rified. She looked down into the lamp and the light flooded
up in her face. Slowly she raised the shears and placed them
inside her dress.

The tapping continued on the door. She heard the voice
calling to her. She leaned over the lamp for a moment and
then suddenly she blew out the light. The room was dark
except for a spot of red that came from the coal stove. She
opened the door. Her voice was strained and sweet. She
called, "I'm coming, Lieutenant, I'm coming!"

7

In the dark, clear night a white, half-withered moon brought little light. The wind was dry and singing over the snow, a quiet wind that blew steadily, evenly from the cold point of the Pole. Over the land the snow lay very deep and dry as sand. The houses snuggled down in the hollows of banked snow, and their windows were dark and shuttered against the cold, and only a little smoke rose from the banked fires.

In the town the footpaths were frozen hard and packed hard. And the streets were silent, too, except when the miserable, cold patrol came by. The houses were dark against the night, and a little lingering warmth remained in the houses against the morning. Near the mine entrance the guards watched the sky and trained their instruments on the sky and turned their listening-instruments against the sky, for it was a clear night for bombing. On nights like this the feathered steel spindles came whistling down and roared to splinters. The land would be visible from the sky tonight, even though the moon seemed to throw little light.

Down toward one end of the village, among the small houses, a dog complained about the cold and the loneliness. He raised his nose to his god and gave a long and fulsome account of the state of the world as it applied to him. He was a practiced singer with a full bell throat and great versatility of range and control. The six men of the patrol slogging dejectedly up and down the streets heard the singing of the dog, and one of the muffled soldiers said, "Seems to me he's getting worse every night. I suppose we ought to shoot him."

And another answered, "Why? Let him howl. He sounds good to me. I used to have a dog at home that howled. I never could break him. Yellow dog. I don't mind the howl. They took my dog when they took the others," he said factually, in a dull voice.

And the corporal said, "Couldn't have dogs eating up food that was needed."

"Oh, I'm not complaining. I know it was necessary. I can't plan the way the leaders do. It seems funny to me, though, that some people here have dogs, and they don't have even as much food as we have. They're pretty gaunt, though, dogs and people."

"They're fools," said the corporal. "That's why they lost so quickly. They can't plan the way we can."

"I wonder if we'll have dogs again after it's over," said the soldier. "I suppose we could get them from America or some place and start the breeds again. What kind of dogs do you suppose they have in America?"

"I don't know," said the corporal. "Probably dogs as crazy as everything else they have." And he went on, "Maybe dogs are no good, anyway. It might be just as well if we never bothered with them, except for police work."

"It might be," said the soldier. "I've heard the Leader doesn't like dogs. I've heard they make him itch and sneeze."

"You hear all kinds of things," the corporal said. "Listen!" The patrol stopped and from a great distance came the bee hum of planes.

"There they come," the corporal said. "Well, there aren't any lights. It's been two weeks, hasn't it, since they came before?"

"Twelve days," said the soldier.

The guards at the mine heard the high drone of the planes. "They're flying high," a sergeant said. And Captain Loft tilted his head back so that he could see under the rim of his helmet. "I judge over 20,000 feet," he said. "Maybe they're going on over."

"Aren't very many." The sergeant listened. "I don't think there are more than three of them. Shall I call the battery?"

"Just see they're alert, and then call Colonel Lanser—no, don't call him. Maybe they aren't coming here. They're nearly over and they haven't started to dive yet."

"Sounds to me like they're circling. I don't think there are more than two," the sergeant said.

In their beds the people heard the planes and they squirmed deep into their featherbeds and listened. In the palace of the Mayor the little sound awakened Colonel Lanser, and he turned over on his back and looked at the dark ceiling with wide-open eyes, and he held his breath to listen better and then his heart beat so that he could not hear as well as he could when he was breathing. Mayor Orden heard the planes in his sleep and they made a dream for him and he moved and whispered in his sleep.

High in the air the two bombers circled, mud-colored planes. They cut their throttles and soared, circling. And from the belly of each one tiny little objects dropped, hundreds of them, one after another. They plummeted a few feet and then little parachutes opened and drifted small packages silently and slowly downward toward the earth, and the planes raised their throttles and gained altitude, and then cut their throttles and circled again, and more of the little objects plummeted down, and then the planes turned and flew back in the direction from which they had come.

The tiny parachutes floated like thistledown and the breeze spread them out and distributed them as seeds on the ends of thistledown are distributed. They drifted so slowly and landed so gently that sometimes the ten-inch packages of dynamite stood upright in the snow, and the little parachutes folded gently down around them. They looked black against the snow. They landed in the white fields and among the woods of the hills and they landed in trees and hung down from the branches. Some of them landed on the housetops of the little town, some in the small front yards, and one landed and stood upright in the snow crown on top of the head of the village statue of St. Albert the Missionary.

One of the little parachutes came down in the street ahead of the patrol and the sergeant said, "Careful! It's a time bomb."

"It ain't big enough," a soldier said.

"Well, don't go near it." The sergeant had his flashlight out and he turned it on the object, a little parachute no bigger than a handkerchief, colored light blue, and hanging from it a package wrapped in blue paper.

"Now don't anybody touch it," the sergeant said. "Harry, you go down to the mine and get the captain. We'll keep an eye on this damn thing."

The late dawn came and the people moving out of their houses in the country saw the spots of blue against the snow. They went to them and picked them up. They unwrapped the paper and read the printed words. They saw the gift and suddenly each finder grew furtive, and he concealed the long tube under his coat and went to some secret place and hid the tube.

And word got to the children about the gift and they combed the countryside in a terrible Easter egg hunt, and when some lucky child saw the blue color, he rushed to the prize and opened it and then he hid the tube and told his parents about it. There were some people who were frightened, who turned the tubes over to the military, but they were not very many. And the soldiers scurried about the town in another Easter egg hunt, but they were not so good at it as the children were.

In the drawing-room of the palace of the Mayor the dining-table remained with the chairs about as it had been placed the day Alex Morden was shot. The room had not the grace it had when it was still the palace of the Mayor. The walls, bare of standing chairs, looked very blank. The table with a few papers scattered about on it made the room look like a business office. The clock on the mantel struck nine. It was a dark day now, overcast with clouds, for the dawn had brought the heavy snow clouds.

Annie came out of the Mayor's room; she swooped by the table and glanced at the papers that lay there. Captain Loft came in. He stopped in the doorway, seeing Annie.

"What are you doing here?" he demanded.

And Annie said sullenly, "Yes, sir."

"I said, what are you doing here?"

"I thought to clean up, sir."

"Let things alone, and go along."

And Annie said, "Yes, sir," and she waited until he was clear of the door, and she scuttled out.

Captain Loft turned back through the doorway and he said, "All right, bring it in." A soldier came through the door behind him, his rifle hung over his shoulder by a strap, and in his arms he held a number of the blue packages, and from the ends of the packages there dangled the little strings and pieces of blue cloth.

Loft said, "Put them on the table." The soldier gingerly laid the packages down. "Now go upstairs and report to Colonel Lanser that I'm here with the—things," and the soldier wheeled about and left the room.

Loft went to the table and picked up one of the packages, and his face wore a look of distaste. He held up the little blue cloth parachute, held it above his head and dropped it, and the cloth opened and the package floated to the floor. He picked up the package again and examined it.

Now Colonel Lanser came quickly into the room, followed by Major Hunter. Hunter was carrying a square of yellow paper in his hand. Lanser said, "Good morning, Captain," and he went to the head of the table and sat down. For a moment he looked at the little pile of tubes, and then he picked one up and held it in his hand. "Sit down, Hunter," he said. "Have you examined these?"

Hunter pulled out a chair and sat down. He looked at the yellow paper in his hand. "Not very carefully," he said. "There are three breaks in the railroad all within ten miles."

"Well, take a look at them and see what you think," Lanser said.

Hunter reached for a tube and stripped off the outer covering, and inside was a small package next to the tube. Hunter took out a knife and cut into the tube. Captain Loft looked over his shoulder. Then Hunter smelled the cut and rubbed his fingers together, and he said, "It's silly. It's commercial dynamite. I don't know what per cent of nitroglycerin until I test it." He looked at the end. "It has a regular dynamite cap, fulminate of mercury, and a fuse—about a minute, I suppose." He tossed the tube back onto the table. "It's very cheap and very simple," he said.

The colonel looked at Loft. "How many do you think were dropped?"

"I don't know, sir," said Loft. "We picked up about fifty of them, and about ninety parachutes they came in. For some reason the people leave the parachutes when they take the tubes, and then there are probably a lot we haven't found yet."

Lanser waved his hand. "It doesn't really matter," he said. "They can drop as many as they want. We can't stop it, and we can't use it against them, either. They haven't conquered anybody."

Loft said fiercely, "We can beat them off the face of the earth!"

Hunter was prying the copper cap out of the top of one of the sticks, and Lanser said, "Yes—we can do that. Have you looked at this wrapper, Hunter?"

"Not yet, I haven't had time."

"It's kind of devilish, this thing," said Colonel Lanser. "The wrapper is blue, so that it's easy to see. Unwrap the outer paper and here"—he picked up the small package— "here is a piece of chocolate. Everybody will be looking for it. I'll bet our own soldiers steal the chocolate. Why, the kids will be looking for them, like Easter eggs."

A soldier came in and laid a square of yellow paper in front of the colonel and retired, and Lanser glanced at it and laughed harshly. "Here's something for you, Hunter. Two more breaks in your line."

Hunter looked up from the copper cap he was examining, and he asked, "How general is this? Did they drop them everywhere?"

Lanser was puzzled. "Now, that's the funny thing. I've talked to the capital. This is the only place they've dropped them."

"What do you make of that?" Hunter asked.

"Well, it's hard to say. I think this is a test place. I suppose if it works here they'll use it all over, and if it doesn't work here they won't bother."

"What are you going to do?" Hunter asked.

"The capital orders me to stamp this out so ruthlessly that they won't drop it any place else."

Hunter said plaintively, "How am I going to mend five breaks in the railroad? I haven't rails right now for five breaks."

"You'll have to rip out some of the old sidings, I guess," said Lanser.

Hunter said, "That'll make a hell of a roadbed."

"Well, anyway, it will make a roadbed."

Major Hunter tossed the tube he had torn apart onto the pile, and Loft broke in, "We must stop this thing at once, sir. We must arrest and punish people who pick these things up, before they use them. We have to get busy so these people won't think we are weak."

Lanser was smiling at him, and he said, "Take it easy, Captain. Let's see what we have first, and then we'll think of remedies."

He took a new package from the pile and unwrapped it. He took the little piece of chocolate, tasted it, and he said, "This is a devilish thing. It's good chocolate, too. I can't even resist it myself. The prize in the grab-bag." Then he picked up the dynamite. "What do you think of this really, Hunter?"

"What I told you. It's very cheap and very effective for small jobs, dynamite with a cap and a one-minute fuse. It's good if you know how to use it. It's no good if you don't."

Lanser studied the print on the inside of the wrapper. "Have you read this?"

"Glanced at it," said Hunter.

"Well, I have read it, and I want you to listen to it carefully," said Lanser. He read from the paper, " 'To the unconquered people: Hide this. Do not expose yourself. You will need this later. It is a present from your friends to you and from you to the invader of your country. Do not try to do large things with it.' " He began to skip through the bill. "Now here, 'rails in the country.' And, 'work at night.' And, 'tie up transportation.' Now here, 'Instructions: rails. Place stick under rail close to the joint, and tight against a tie. Pack mud or hard-beaten snow around it so that it is firm. When the fuse is lighted you have a slow count of sixty before it explodes.' "

He looked up at Hunter and Hunter said simply, "It works." Lanser looked back at his paper and he skipped through. " 'Bridges: Weaken, do not destroy.' And here, 'transmission poles,' and here, 'culverts, trucks.' " He laid the blue handbill down. "Well, there it is."

Loft said angrily, "We must do something! There must be a way to control this. What does headquarters say?"

Lanser pursed his lips and his fingers played with one of the tubes. "I could have told you what they'd say before they said it. I have the orders. 'Set booby traps and poison the chocolate.' " He paused for a moment and then he said, "Hunter, I'm a good, loyal man, but sometimes when I hear the brilliant ideas of headquarters, I wish I were a civilian, an old, crippled civilian. They always think they are dealing with stupid people. I don't say that this is a measure of their intelligence, do I?"

Hunter looked amused. "Do you?"

Lanser said sharply, "No, I don't. But what will happen? One man will pick up one of these and get blown to bits by our booby trap. One kid will eat chocolate and die of strychnine poisoning. And then?" He looked down at his hands. "They will poke them with poles, or lasso them, before they touch them. They will try the chocolate on the cat. Goddamn it, Major, these are intelligent people. Stupid traps won't catch them twice."

Loft cleared his throat. "Sir, this is defeatist talk," he said. "We must do something. Why do you suppose it was only dropped here, sir?"

And Lanser said, "For one of two reasons: either this town was picked at random or else there is communication between this town and the outside. We know that some of the young men have got away."

Loft repeated dully, "We must do something, sir."

Now Lanser turned on him. "Loft, I think I'll recommend you for the General Staff. You want to get to work before you even know what the problem is. This is a new kind of conquest. Always before, it was possible to disarm a people and keep them in ignorance. Now they listen to their radios and we can't stop them. We can't even find their radios."

A soldier looked in through the doorway. "Mr. Corell to see you, sir."

Lanser replied, "Tell him to wait." He continued to talk to Loft. "They read the handbills; weapons drop from the sky for them. Now it's dynamite, Captain. Pretty soon it may be grenades, and then poison."

Loft said anxiously, "They haven't dropped poison yet."

"No, but they will. Can you think what will happen to the morale of our men or even to you if the people had some of those little game darts, you know, those silly things you throw at a target, the points coated perhaps with cyanide, silent, deadly little things that you couldn't hear coming, that would pierce the uniform and make no noise? And what if our men knew that arsenic was about? Would you or they drink or eat comfortably?"

Hunter said dryly, "Are you writing the enemy's campaign, Colonel?"

"No, I'm trying to anticipate it."

Loft said, "Sir, we sit here talking when we should be searching for this dynamite. If there is organization among these people, we have to find it, we have to stamp it out."

"Yes," said Lanser, "we have to stamp it out, ferociously, I suppose. You take a detail, Loft. Get Prackle to take one. I wish we had more junior officers. Tonder's getting killed didn't help us a bit. Why couldn't he let women alone?"

Loft said, "I don't like the way Lieutenant Prackle is acting, sir."

"What's he doing?"

"He isn't doing anything, but he's jumpy and he's gloomy."

"Yes," Lanser said, "I know. It's a thing I've talked about so much. You know," he said, "I might be a major-general if I hadn't talked about it so much. We trained our young men for victory and you've got to admit they're glorious in victory, but they don't quite know how to act in defeat. We told them they were brighter and braver than other young men. It was a kind of shock to them to find out that they aren't a bit braver or brighter than other young men."

Loft said harshly, "What do you mean by defeat? We are not defeated?"

And Lanser looked coldly up at him for a long moment and did not speak, and finally Loft's eyes wavered, and he said, "Sir."

"Thank you," said Lanser.

"You don't demand it of the others, sir."

"They don't think about it, so it isn't an insult. When you leave it out, it's insulting."   .

"Yes, sir," said Loft.

"Go on, now, try to keep Prackle in hand. Start your search. I don't want any shooting unless there's an overt act, do you understand?"

"Yes, sir," said Loft, and he saluted formally and went out of the room.

Hunter regarded Colonel Lanser amusedly. "Weren't you rough on him?"

"I had to be. He's frightened. I know his kind. He has to be disciplined when he's afraid or he'll go to pieces. He relies on discipline the way other men rely on sympathy. I suppose you'd better get to your rails. You might as well expect that tonight is the time when they'll really blow them, though."

Hunter stood up and he said, "Yes. I suppose the orders are coming in from the capital?"

"Yes."

"Are they—"

"You know what they are," Lanser interrupted. "You know what they'd have to be. Take the leaders, shoot the leaders, take hostages, shoot the hostages, take more hostages, shoot them"—his voice had risen but now it sank almost to a whisper—"and the hatred growing and the hurt between us deeper and deeper."

Hunter hesitated. "Have they condemned any from the list of names?" and he motioned slightly toward the Mayor's bedroom.

Lanser shook his head. "No, not yet. They are just arrested so far."

Hunter said quietly, "Colonel, do you want me to recommend—maybe you're overtired, Colonel? Could I—you know—could I report that you're overtired?"

For a moment Lanser covered his eyes with his hand, and then his shoulders straightened and his face grew hard. "I'm not a civilian, Hunter. We're short enough of officers already. You know that. Get to your work, Major. I have to see Corell."

Hunter smiled. He went to the door and opened it, and he said out of the door, "Yes, he's here," and over his shoulder he said to Lanser, "It's Prackle. He wants to see you."

"Send him in," said Lanser.

Prackle came in, his face sullen, belligerent. "Colonel Lanser, sir, I wish to—"

"Sit down," said Lanser. "Sit down and rest a moment. Be a good soldier, Lieutenant."

The stiffness went out of Prackle quickly. He sat down beside the table and rested his elbows on it. "I wish—"

And Lanser said, "Don't talk for a moment. I know what

it is. You didn't think it would be this way, did you? You thought it would be rather nice."

"They hate us," Prackle said. "They hate us so much."

Lanser smiled. "I wonder if I know what it is. It takes young men to make good soldiers, and young men need young women, is that it?"

"Yes, that's it."

"Well," Lanser said kindly, "does she hate you?"

Prackle looked at him in amazement. "I don't know, sir. Sometimes I think she's only sorry."

"And you're pretty miserable?"

"I don't like it here, sir."

"No, you thought it would be fun, didn't you? Lieutenant Tonder went to pieces and then he went out and they got a knife in him. I could send you home. Do you want to be sent home, knowing we need you here?"

Prackle said uneasily, "No, sir, I don't."

"Good. Now I'll tell you, and I hope you'll understand it. You're not a man any more. You are a soldier. Your comfort is of no importance and, Lieutenant, your life isn't of much importance. If you live, you will have memories. That's about all you will have. Meanwhile you must take orders and carry them out. Most of the orders will be unpleasant, but that's not your business. I will not lie to you, Lieutenant. They should have trained you for this, and not for flower-strewn streets. They should have built your soul with truth, not led along with lies." His voice grew hard. "But you took the job, Lieutenant. Will you stay with it or quit it? We can't take care of your soul."

Prackle stood up. "Thank you, sir."

"And the girl," Lanser continued, "the girl, Lieutenant, you may rape her, or protect her, or marry her—that is of no importance so long as you shoot her when it is ordered."

Prackle said wearily, "Yes, sir, thank you, sir."

"I assure you it is better to know. I assure you of that. It is better to know. Go now, Lieutenant, and if Corell is still waiting, send him in." And he watched Lieutenant Prackle out of the doorway.

When Mr. Corell came in, he was a changed man. His left arm was in a cast, and he was no longer the jovial, friendly, smiling Corell. His face was sharp and bitter, and his eyes squinted down like little dead pig's eyes.

"I should have come before, Colonel," he said, "but your lack of co-operation made me hesitant."

Lanser said, "You were waiting for a reply to your report, I remember."

"I was waiting for much more than that. You refused me a position of authority. You said I was valueless. You did not realize that I was in this town long before you were. You left the Mayor in his office, contrary to my advice."

Lanser said, "Without him here we might have had more disorder than we have."

"That is a matter of opinion," Corell said. "This man is a leader of a rebellious people."

"Nonsense," said Lanser; "he's just a simple man."

With his good hand Corell took a black notebook from his right pocket and opened it with his fingers. "You forgot, Colonel, that I had my sources, that I had been here a long time before you. I have to report to you that Mayor Orden has been in constant contact with every happening in this community. On the night when Lieutenant Tonder was murdered, he was in the house where the murder was committed. When the girl escaped to the hills, she stayed with one of his relatives. I traced her there, but she was gone. Whenever men have escaped, Orden has known about it and has helped them. And I even strongly suspect that he is somewhere in the picture of these little parachutes."

Lanser said eagerly, "But you can't prove it."

"No," Corell said, "I can't prove it. The first thing I know; the last I only suspect. Perhaps now you will be willing to listen to me."

Lanser said quietly, "What do you suggest?"

"These suggestions, Colonel, are a little stronger than suggestions. Orden must now be a hostage and his life must depend on the peacefulness of this community. His life must depend on the lighting of one single fuse on one single stick of dynamite."

He reached into his pocket again and brought out a little folding book, and he flipped it open and laid it in front of the colonel. "This, sir, was the answer to my report from headquarters. You will notice that it gives me certain authority."

Lanser looked at the little book and he spoke quietly. "You really did go over my head, didn't you?" He looked up at Corell with frank dislike in his eyes. "I heard you'd been injured. How did it happen?"

Corell said, "On the night when your lieutenant was murdered I was waylaid. The patrol saved me. Some of the townsmen escaped in my boat that night. Now, Colonel, must I express more strongly than I have that Mayor Orden must be held hostage?"

Lanser said, "He is here, he hasn't escaped. How can we hold him more hostage than we are?"

Suddenly in the distance there was a sound of an explosion, and both men looked around in the direction from which it came. Corell said, "There it is, Colonel, and you know perfectly well that if this experiment succeeds there will be dynamite in every invaded country."

Lanser repeated quietly, "What do you suggest?"

"Just what I have said. Orden must be held against rebellion."

"And if they rebel and we shoot Orden?"

"Then that little doctor is next; although he holds no position, he's next authority in the town."

"But he holds no office."

"He has the confidence of the people."

"And when we shoot him, what then?"

"Then we have authority. Then rebellion will be broken. When we have killed the leaders, the rebellion will be broken."

Lanser asked quizzically, "Do you really think so?"

"It must be so."

Lanser shook his head slowly and then he called, "Sentry!" The door opened and a soldier appeared in the doorway. "Sergeant," said Lanser, "I have placed Mayor Orden under arrest, and I have placed Doctor Winter under arrest. You will see to it that Orden is guarded and you will bring Winter here immediately."

The sentry said, "Yes, sir."

Lanser looked up at Corell and he said, "You know, I hope you know what you're doing. I do hope you know what you're doing."

8

In the little town the news ran quickly. It was communicated by whispers in doorways, by quick, meaningful looks—"The Mayor's been arrested"—and through the town a little quiet jubilance ran, a fierce little jubilance, and people talked quietly together and went apart, and people going in to buy food leaned close to the clerks for a moment and a word passed between them.

The people went into the country, into the woods, searching for dynamite. And children playing in the snow found the dynamite, and by now even the children had their instructions. They opened the packages and ate the chocolate, and then they buried the dynamite in the snow and told their parents where it was.

Far out in the country a man picked up a tube and read the instructions and he said to himself, "I wonder if this works." He stood the tube up in the snow and lighted the fuse, and he ran back from it and counted, but his count was fast. It was sixty-eight before the dynamite exploded. He said, "It does work," and he went hurriedly about looking for more tubes.

Almost as though at a signal the people went into their houses and the doors were closed, the streets were quiet. At the mine the soldiers carefully searched every miner who went into the shaft, searched and re-searched, and the soldiers were nervous and rough and they spoke harshly to the miners. The miners looked coldly at them, and behind their eyes was a little fierce jubilance.

In the drawing-room of the palace of the Mayor the table had been cleaned up, and a soldier stood guard at Mayor Orden's bedroom door. Annie was on her knees in front of the coal grate, putting little pieces of coal on the fire. She looked up at the sentry standing in front of Mayor Orden's door and she said truculently, "Well, what are you going to do to him?" The soldier did not answer.

The outside door opened and another soldier came in, holding Doctor Winter by the arm. He closed the door behind Doctor Winter and stood against the door inside the room. Doctor Winter said, "Hello, Annie, how's His Excellency?"

And Annie pointed at the bedroom and said, "He's in there."

"He isn't ill?" Doctor Winter said.

"No, he didn't seem to be," said Annie. "I'll see if I can tell him you're here." She went to the sentry and spoke imperiously. "Tell His Excellency that Doctor Winter is here, do you hear me?"

The sentry did not answer and did not move, but behind him the door opened and Mayor Orden stood in the doorway. He ignored the sentry and brushed past him and stepped into the room. For a moment the sentry considered taking him back, and then he returned to his place beside the door. Orden said, "Thank you, Annie. Don't go too far away, will you? I might need you."

Annie said, "No, sir, I won't. Is Madame all right?"

"She's doing her hair. Do you want to see her, Annie?"

"Yes, sir," said Annie, and she brushed past the sentry, too, and went into the bedroom and shut the door.

Orden said, "Is there something you want, Doctor?"

Winter grinned sardonically and pointed over his shoulder to his guard. "Well, I guess I'm under arrest. My friend here brought me."

Orden said, "I suppose it was bound to come. What will they do now, I wonder?" And the two men looked at each other for a long time and each one knew what the other one was thinking.

And then Orden continued as though he had been talking. "You know, I couldn't stop it if I wanted to."

"I know," said Winter, "but they don't know." And he went on with a thought he had been having. "A time-minded people," he said, "and the time is nearly up. They think that just because they have only one leader and one head, we are all like that. They know that ten heads lopped off will destroy them, but we are a free people; we have as many heads as we have people, and in a time of need leaders pop up among us like mushrooms."

Orden put his hand on Winter's shoulder and he said, "Thank you. I knew it, but it's good to hear you say it. The little people won't go under, will they?" He searched Winter's face anxiously.

And the doctor reassured him, "Why, no, they won't. As a matter of fact, they will grow stronger with outside help."

The room was silent for a moment. The sentry shifted his position a little and his rifle clinked on a button.

Orden said, "I can talk to you, Doctor, and I probably won't be able to talk again. There are little shameful things in my mind." He coughed and glanced at the rigid soldier, but the soldier gave no sign of having heard. "I have been thinking of my own death. If they follow the usual course, they must kill me, and then they must kill you." And when Winter was silent, he said, "Mustn't they?"

"Yes, I guess so." Winter walked to one of the gilt chairs, and as he was about to sit down he noticed that its tapestry was torn, and he petted the seat with his fingers as though that would mend it. And he sat down gently because it was torn.

And Orden went on, "You know, I'm afraid, I have been thinking of ways to escape, to get out of it. I have been thinking of running away. I have been thinking of pleading for my life, and it makes me ashamed."

And Winter, looking up, said, "But you haven't done it."

"No, I haven't."

"And you won't do it."

Orden hesitated. "No, I won't. But I have thought of it."

And Winter said, gently, "How do you know everyone doesn't think of it? How do you know I haven't thought of it?"

"I wonder why they arrested you, too," Orden said. "I guess they will have to kill you, too."

"I guess so," said Winter. He rolled his thumbs and watched them tumble over and over.

"You know so." Orden was silent for a moment and then he said, "You know, Doctor, I am a little man and this is a little town, but there must be a spark in little men that can burst into flame. I am afraid, I am terribly afraid, and I thought of all the things I might do to save my own life, and then that went away, and sometimes now I feel a kind of exultation, as though I were bigger and better than I am, and do you know what I have been thinking, Doctor?" He smiled, remembering. "Do you remember in school, in the *Apology*? Do you remember Socrates says, 'Someone will say, "And are you not ashamed, Socrates, of a course of life which is likely to bring you to an untimely end?" To him I may fairly answer, "There you are mistaken: a man who is good for anything ought not to calculate the chance of living or dying; he ought only to consider whether he is doing right or wrong."'" Orden paused, trying to remember.

Doctor Winter sat tensely forward now, and he went on with it, "'Acting the part of a good man or of a bad.' I don't think you have it quite right. You never were a good scholar. You were wrong in the denunciation, too."

Orden chuckled. "Do you remember that?"

"Yes," said Winter, eagerly, "I remember it well. You forgot a line or a word. It was graduation, and you were so excited you forgot to tuck in your shirt-tail and your shirt-tail was out. You wondered why they laughed."

Orden smiled to himself, and his hand went secretly behind him and patrolled for a loose shirt-tail. "I was Socrates," he said, "and I denounced the School Board. How I denounced them! I bellowed it, and I could see them grow red."

Winter said, "They were holding their breaths to keep from laughing. Your shirt-tail was out."

Mayor Orden laughed. "How long ago? Forty years?"

"Forty-six."

The sentry by the bedroom door moved quietly over to the sentry by the outside door. They spoke softly out of the corners of their mouths like children whispering in school. "How long you been on duty?"

"All night. Can't hardly keep my eyes open."

"Me too. Hear from your wife on the boat yesterday?"

"Yes! She said say hello tó you. Said she heard you was wounded. She don't write much."

"Tell her I'm all right."

"Sure—when I write."

The Mayor raised his head and looked at the ceiling and he muttered, "Um—um—um. I wonder if I can remember—how does it go?"

And Winter prompted him, " 'And now, O men—' "

And Orden said softly, " 'And now, O men who have condemned me—' "

Colonel Lanser came quietly into the room; the sentries stiffened. Hearing the words, the colonel stopped and listened.

Orden looked at the ceiling, lost in trying to remember

the old words. " 'And now, O men who have condemned me,' " he said, " 'I would fain prophesy to you—for I am about to die—and—in the hour of death—men are gifted with prophetic power. And I—prophesy to you who are my murderers—that immediately after my—my death—' "

And Winter stood up, saying, "Departure."

Orden looked at him. "What?"

And Winter said, "The word is 'departure,' not 'death.' You made the same mistake before. You made that mistake forty-six years ago."

"No, it is death. It is death." Orden looked around and saw Colonel Lanser watching him. He asked, "Isn't it 'death'?"

Colonel Lanser said, " 'Departure.' It is 'immediately after my departure.' "

Doctor Winter insisted, "You see, that's two against one. 'Departure' is the word. It is the same mistake you made before."

Then Orden looked straight ahead and his eyes were in his memory, seeing nothing outward. And he went on, " 'I prophesy to you who are my murderers that immediately after my—departure punishment far heavier than you have inflicted on me will surely await you.' "

Winter nodded encouragingly, and Colonel Lanser nodded, and they seemed to be trying to help him to remember. And Orden went on, " 'Me you have killed because you wanted to escape the accuser, and not to give an account of your lives—!' "

Lieutenant Prackle entered excitedly, crying, "Colonel Lanser!"

Colonel Lanser said, "Shh—" and he held out his hand to restrain him.

And Orden went on softly, " 'But that will not be as you suppose; far otherwise.' " His voice grew stronger. " 'For I say that there will be more accusers of you than there are now' "—he made a little gesture with his hand, a speech-making gesture—" 'accusers whom hitherto I have restrained; and as they are younger they will be more inconsiderate with you, and you will be more offended at them.' " He frowned, trying to remember.

And Lieutenant Prackle said, "Colonel Lanser, we have found some men with dynamite."

And Lanser said, "Hush."

Orden continued, " 'If you think that by killing men you can prevent someone from censuring your evil lives, you are mistaken.' " He frowned and thought and he looked at the ceiling, and he smiled embarrassedly and he said, "That's all I can remember. It is gone away from me."

And Doctor Winter said, "It's very good after forty-six years, and you weren't very good at it forty-six years ago."

Lieutenant Prackle broke in, "The men have dynamite, Colonel Lanser."

"Did you arrest them?"

"Yes, sir. Captain Loft and—"

Lanser said, "Tell Captain Loft to guard them." He re-captured himself and he advanced into the room and he said, "Orden, these things must stop."

And the Mayor smiled helplessly at him. "They cannot stop, sir."

Colonel Lanser said harshly, "I arrested you as a hostage for the good behavior of your people. Those are my orders."

"But that won't stop it," Orden said simply. "You don't understand. When I have become a hindrance to the people, they will do without me."

Lanser said, "Tell me truly what you think. If the people know you will be shot if they light another fuse, what will they do?"

The Mayor looked helplessly at Doctor Winter. And then

the bedroom door opened and Madame came out, carrying the Mayor's chain of office in her hand. She said, "You forgot this."

Orden said, "What? Oh, yes,." and he stooped his head and Madame slipped the chain of office over his head, and he said, "Thank you, dear."

Madame complained, "You always forget it. You forget it all the time."

The Mayor looked at the end of the chain he held in his hand—the gold medallion with the insignia of his office carved on it. Lanser pressed him. "What will they do?"

"I don't know," said the Mayor. "I think they will light the fuse."

"Suppose you ask them not to?"

Winter said, "Colonel, this morning I saw a little boy building a snow man, while three grown soldiers watched to see that he did not caricature your leader. He made a pretty good likeness, too, before they destroyed it."

Lanser ignored the doctor. "Suppose you ask them not to?" he repeated.

Orden seemed half asleep; his eyes were drooped, and he tried to think. He said, "I am not a very brave man, sir. I think they will light it, anyway." He struggled with his speech. "I hope they will, but if I ask them not to, they will be sorry."

Madame said, "What is this all about?"

"Be quiet a moment, dear," the Mayor said.

"But you think they will light it?" Lanser insisted.

The Mayor spoke proudly. "Yes, they will light it. I have no choice of living or dying, you see, sir, but—I do have a choice of how I do it. If I tell them not to fight, they will be sorry, but they will fight. If I tell them to fight, they will be glad, and I who am not a very brave man will have made them a little braver." He smiled apologetically. "You see, it is an easy thing to do, since the end for me is the same."

Lanser said, "If you say yes, we can tell them you said no. We can tell them you begged for your life."

And Winter broke in angrily, "They would know. You do not keep secrets. One of your men got out of hand one night and he said the flies had conquered the flypaper, and now the whole nation knows his words. They have made a song of it. The flies have conquered the flypaper. You do not keep secrets, Colonel."

From the direction of the mine a whistle tooted shrilly. And a quick gust of wind sifted dry snow against the windows.

Orden fingered his gold medallion. He said quietly, "You see, sir, nothing can change it. You will be destroyed and driven out." His voice was very soft. "The people don't like to be conquered, sir, and so they will not be. Free men cannot start a war, but once it is started, they can fight on in defeat. Herd men, followers of a leader, cannot do that, and so it is always the herd men who win battles and the free men who win wars. You will find that is so, sir."

Lanser was erect and stiff. "My orders are clear. Eleven o'clock was the deadline. I have taken hostages. If there is violence, the hostages will be executed."

And Doctor Winter said to the colonel, "Will you carry out the orders, knowing they will fail?"

Lanser's face was tight. "I will carry out my orders no matter what they are, but I do think, sir, a proclamation from you might save many lives."

Madame broke in plaintively, "I wish you would tell me what all this nonsense is."

"It is nonsense, dear."

"But they can't arrest the Mayor," she explained to him.

Orden smiled at her. "No," he said, "they can't arrest the Mayor. The Mayor is an idea conceived by free men. It will escape arrest."

From the distance there was a sound of an explosion. And the echo of it rolled to the hills and back again. The whistle at the coal mine tooted a shrill, sharp warning. Orden stood very tensely for a moment and then he smiled. A second explosion roared—nearer this time and heavier—and its echo rolled back from the mountains. Orden looked at his watch and then he took his watch and chain and put them in Doctor Winter's hand. "How did it go about the flies?" he asked.

"The flies have conquered the flypaper," Winter said.

Orden called, "Annie!" The bedroom door opened instantly and the Mayor said, "Were you listening?"

"Yes, sir." Annie was embarrassed.

And now an explosion roared near by and there was a sound of splintering wood and breaking glass, and the door behind the sentries puffed open. And Orden said, "Annie, I want you to stay with Madame as long as she needs you. Don't leave her alone." He put his arm around Madame and he kissed her on the forehead and then he moved slowly toward the door where Lieutenant Prackle stood. In the doorway he turned back to Doctor Winter. "Crito, I owe a cock to Asclepius," he said tenderly. "Will you remember to pay the debt?"

Winter closed his eyes for a moment before he answered, "The debt shall be paid."

Orden chuckled then. "I remembered that one. I didn't forget that one." He put his hand on Prackle's arm, and the lieutenant flinched away from him.

And Winter nodded slowly. "Yes, you remembered. The debt shall be paid."

First published in Great Britain in 1998 by
Heinemann Library, Halley Court, Jordan Hill, Oxford OX2 8EJ, a division of
Reed Educational and Professional Publishing Limited.

OXFORD MELBOURNE AUCKLAND
JOHANNESBURG BLANTYRE GABORONE
IBADAN PORTSMOUTH (NH) USA CHICAGO

01 00 99 98
10 9 8 7 6 5 4 3 2 1

ISBN 0 431 09096 3 (HB)
ISBN 0 431 09100 5 (PB)

British Library Cataloguing in Publication Data

Brunning, Bob
Heavy metal. – (Sound trackers)
1. Heavy metal (Music) – Juvenile literature
I. Title
781. 6 ' 6

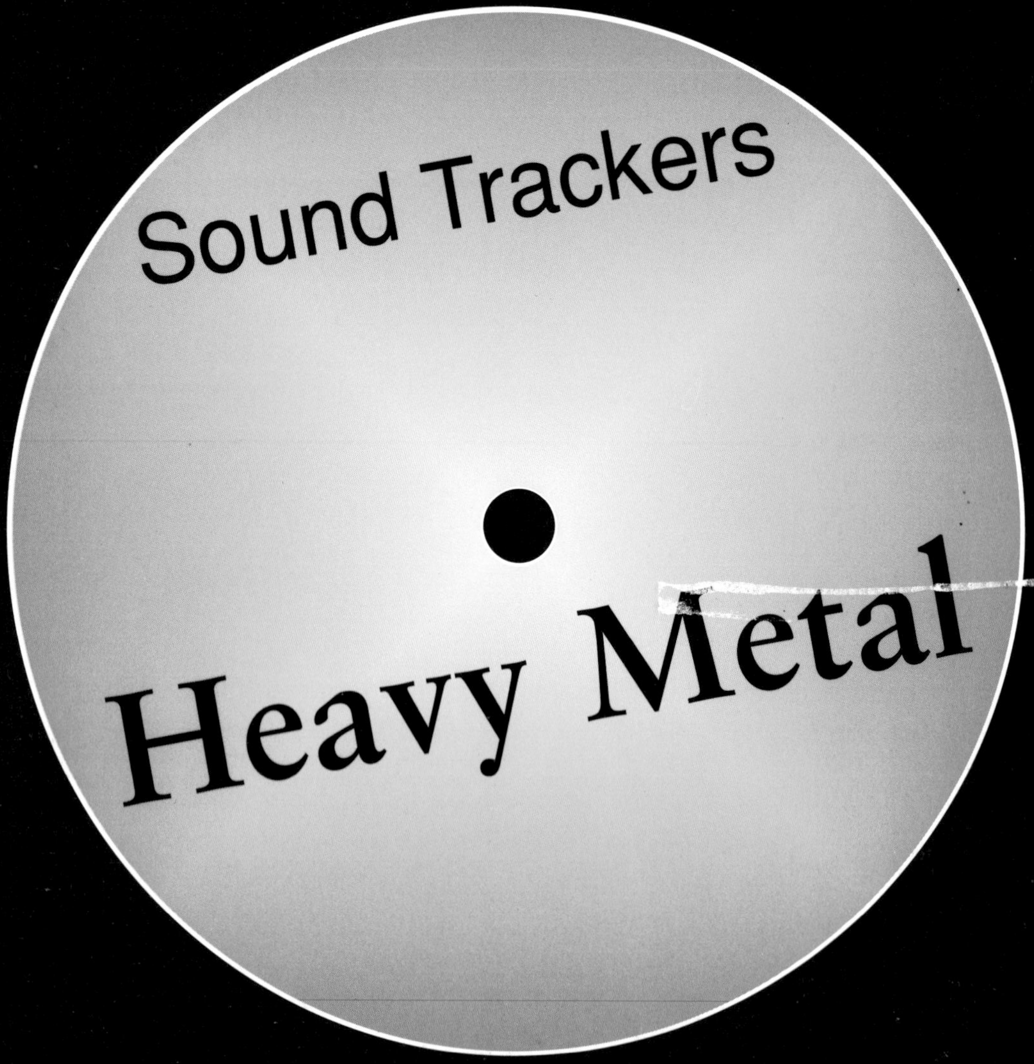
Sound Trackers
Heavy Metal

SOUND TRACKERS

Heavy Metal

Bob Brunning

Heinemann

CONTENTS

On these discs is a selection of the artists' recordings. Many of these albums are now available on CD. If they are not, many of the tracks from them can be found on compilation CDs.

These boxes give you extra information about the music, the artists and performers, and their times. Some contain anecdotes about the artists themselves or the people who helped – or occasionally exploited – them. Others provide historical facts and fascinating insights into the music, lifestyles, fans, fads and fashions of the day.

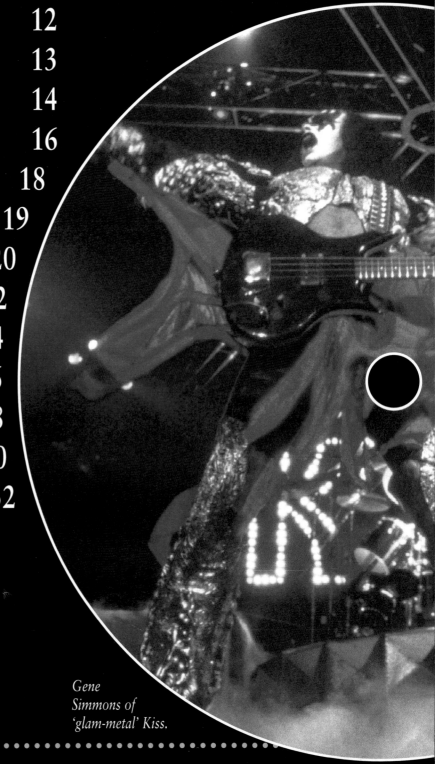

Gene Simmons of 'glam-metal' Kiss.

INTRODUCTION

Some say that heavy metal is the easiest style of
modern music to identify. But those closer to
HM—or "metal"—say that it's the most difficult.
So what, in general, are they talking about?

Phil Lynott of 'folk metal' Thin Lizzy.

First, the name. *Heavy metal* was a phrase in a
1959 novel (see page 7). 'Heavy' means the
sounds are loud and deep. 'Metal' is the
metallic crashing of guitar strings. HM is
usually guitar-led, often with fast, highly
technical playing. Songs may be ponderously slow or thrashingly
fast, with forceful, dramatic vocals, yells and roars.

Next, equipment. Guitars and drums are often customized (see
page 17) . The back line (on-stage amplifiers and speakers for
the band itself) is towering. The public address (sound system
for the audience) is mountainous. Power = volume = energy.

Third, image. Often long hair, leather waistcoats and scruffy
jeans, with plenty of macho posing, guitar waving and clenched
fists. Some HM bands prefer extravagant theatrics, colourful
make-up and glamorous costumes – or sinister darkness.

HM grew out of progressive and heavy rock from the late 1960s,
with bands such as Cream, Led Zeppelin and Deep Purple. From 1976,
Punk brought a competing type of loud, brash music. In the 1980s, some
saw HM as "dinosaur rock". But its bands and fans have fought back, and
heavy metal is once again popular, proud and loud.

AC/DC

Most young people cannot wait to get out of school uniform. Angus Young, guitar-thrashing frontman from one of the first true heavy metal bands, did the reverse. He wore his uniform on stage, even short trousers and a cap! But then, AC/DC always stood by their own decisions. Their classic HM sound has endured for over 20 years.

THE WIZARDS FROM OZ

Often hailed as an Australian band, three key members of AC/DC were actually born in Scotland. Brothers Angus and Malcolm Young founded the band in Sydney, in 1973. Members came and went until 1976, when singer Bon (Ronald) Scott stabilized the line-up. Another Young brother, George – who had achieved success with the Easybeats' pop classic 'Friday On My Mind' – helped set up a recording contract with Australian company Albert. But the first three albums and seven singles, released only in Australia, hardly set the rock scene on fire.

ROCK THE WORLD

Nevertheless, the band had confidence in its loud, high-energy stage act. To achieve true stardom, they decided to spread out from Australia. In 1977, with Mark Evans (bass) and Phil Rudd (drums), they recorded 'Let There Be Rock'.

Angus Young plays lead guitar.

Then, with Cliff Williams (of Romford, Essex) replacing Evans, they toured Europe and North America. Success! The album entered the Top 20 in December. 1978's 'Powerage' did less well, but the next year's 'Highway To Hell' blasted into the Top 10. However, disaster struck on 20 February 1980 when Scott choked to death after heavy drinking. After some soul searching, the rest of AC/DC bravely decided to carry on and signed up Brian Johnson, whose vocals were uncannily like Scott's.

A LIKING FOR LEATHER

The phrase *heavy metal* was derived from a quote by William Burroughs, about 'heavy metal thunder', in his 1959 novel *The Naked Lunch*. Soon HM became associated with other dark, strong, tough, powerful, macho-style 'heavy' subjects such as motorcycles, leather clothes, chrome, chains and semi-military uniforms. The 1970s trend towards 'glam' brought sparkle, glitter, make-up and a slightly more camp or effeminate image. This was adopted by some HM performers. But the basic heavy leather look is still generally popular, with HM artists and followers alike.

Judas Priest, popular from the late '70s to about 1990, model the HM leather look.

BACK TO BLACK HITS

1980 also saw AC/DC's first No. 1 album, 'Back In Black'. In '81 'For Those Who Are About To Rock (We Salute You)' sold massively, and a scorching performance at HM's premier festival, Castle Donington, established AC/DC as one of the world's top heavy metal bands. There have been personnel changes since, but Top 10 albums continue to flow, including 'Live' which topped video sales too. The Youngs and Johnson continue to rock, and Angus still has not grown out of his school uniform ...

Johnson's trademark is a flat cloth cap.

'Let There Be Rock'
October '77
'Highway To Hell'
August '79
'Back In Black' July '80
'For Those About To Rock (We Salute You)'
November '81

'Flick Of The Switch' August '83
'The Razor's Edge' October '90
'Box Set' August '91
'Live' October '92
'Ballbreaker'
September '95

AEROSMITH

Any type of music has its purer and simpler styles, and its more complicated, involved ones. Aerosmith combine both. They are one of the cleverer, more tricksy HM bands, with lengthy songs arranged into various linked sections, and rapid changes of pace and rhythm that swap keys and riffs at speed. Some people would argue that they are not truly 'metal'. They are heavy rock, and too clever for their own boots ...

EARLY PROBLEMS

Joey Kramer, Aerosmith's drummer from the beginning, came up with the band name by mixing letters in the style of the board word game Scrabble. Joey, with vocalist Steven Tyler and guitarist Joe Perry, considered two possibilities – Songsmith and Aerospace. They mixed the two and luckily chose the better combination. The band's first incarnation was as a fairly standard heavy rock outfit in the late 1970s. But drink and drugs took their toll. Aerosmith's career began to falter during the 1980s. The songwriting duo of Tyler and Perry lost their knack of creating tunes which were tough yet smart.

Substance abuse earned songwriters Tyler (left) and Perry (right) the nickname of 'Toxic Twins'.

WAKING UP

Despite their problems, Aerosmith have boasted an exceptionally stable line-up over many years. Natural frontman Tyler on vocals, keyboards and other instruments, plus the thoughtful Perry and super-rapid drummer Kramer, are accompanied by Brad Whitford on rhythm guitar and Tom Hamilton on bass. In 1987 'Permanent Vacation' showed a newer, sharper version of the band. The same year rappers Run DMC had a huge hit single with 'Walk This Way'. The song had been written by Tyler and Perry, and had featured on an earlier Aerosmith recording.

'Permanent Vacation'
August '87
'Pump'
September '89
'Get A Grip'
April '93

'Big Ones'
November '94
'Nine Lives'
March '97

Girlschool charted in 1981 with 'Hit 'n' Run'.

BETTER, BETTER

Aerosmith developed their theme of heavy-but-clever songs with a vengeance, assisted by a colourful stage show topped by Tyler's tall hat. Their '89 album 'Pump' included the 5-minutes-21-seconds 'Love In An Elevator', an established classic in mini-opera format. It still appears regularly on lists of all-time great rock songs.

The band's fortunes soared with a guest appearance at 'Waynestock' in the cult movie 'Wayne's World 2'. In 1994 a release of earlier tracks reminded listeners that Aerosmith had always harboured talent and showmanship. As some areas of heavy metal become musically more complex, but without losing the essential strong riffs and pounding beats, Aerosmith are elder statesmen who continue to lead from the front.

BLACK SABBATH

Heavy metal is sometimes linked with black magic, curses, spells and the Devil. Partly responsible are one of the 'founding father' bands of HM, still regarded as among the loudest and heaviest. Black Sabbath can hardly argue against the case. Their name was inspired by bassist Terry 'Geezer' Butler's interest in Dennis Wheatley's 1960s novel 'The Devil Rides Out'.

'Black Sabbath'
February '70
'Paranoid' September '70
'Master Of Reality' August '71
'Sabbath Bloody Sabbath'
November '73
'Sabotage' September '75

'Technical Ecstasy' October '76
'Heaven And Hell' April '80
'Live At Last' June '80
'Born Again' September '83
'Dehumaniser'
June '92

CHANGE OF TUNE

In 1967, singer John Michael 'Ozzy' Osbourne joined up with guitarist Tony Iommi, Butler on bass and drummer Bill Ward. Known by various hippie-inspired names such as Mythology and Whole Earth, they dabbled in musical styles such as jazz and blues. But as their own ponderous, riff-laden, pile-driving sound took shape, they adopted the name Black Sabbath, and in 1970 moved to the progressive Vertigo label. Their powerful dark image, immensely loud stage show and relentless touring paid off, and the first album 'Black Sabbath' made Top 10 in March. The

Ozzy Osbourne is still successfully solo in 1998.

single 'Paranoid' from the second chart-topping album of the same name has become an all-time HM classic.

COURTING CONTROVERSY

The Birmingham-based quartet's controversial approach to musical content, including substance abuse and mental illness, led to widespread criticism. The band were accused of encouraging drugs or even suicide. Nevertheless their first six albums (to 1975) made the Top 10, and in 1973 they were joined by ex-Yes keyboardist Rick Wakeman.

Wakeman brought the organ sound.

Gradually success waned, despite exhausting global tours. Musical differences surfaced and Ozzy Osborne left temporarily in late 1977, then for good in '78. American Ronnie James Dio sang on 1978's 'Never Say Die'. In spite of his impressive track record (see page 15), he was gone by 1982, replaced by Ian Gillan. Ward also left, and in came Vinnie Appice, brother of Carmine Appice, acclaimed drummer in Vanilla Fudge. 1983 saw the arrival of keyboard player Geoff Nichols, Glenn Hughes on vocals, bassist Dave Spitz and drummer Eric Singer.

REGROUPING

The musicianship was still first-class, but the magic and fan base were evaporating, with only Tony Iommi from the original group. Another drummer who passed through Sabbath's ranks was the hugely experienced Cozy Powell (see panel, right). In 1991 Iommi attempted to recreate the band's original line-up and persuaded Butler, but drummer Ward refused. With Ronnie James Dio back again, the re-vamped Sabbath entered the Top 30 with 'Tyr' and 'Dehumaniser'. Despite their '90s fade-out, Black Sabbath richly deserve their place as one of HM's all-time greats.

POWELL POWER

Cozy Powell became Black Sabbath's drummer during the late 1980s. In April 1998 he sadly died in a car crash near his Bristol home. Cozy was a phenomenally fast, energetic drummer with a pivotal role in British heavy metal music. In addition to Black Sabbath, he played and recorded with Whitesnake, Rainbow, ELP (Emerson Lake and Powell), Jeff Beck, the Michael Shenker Group, Roger Daltrey and, perhaps surprisingly, '60s folk singer Donovan. He also had single hits – featuring massive drum sounds, of course – including 'Dance With The Devil' in 1973. Powell could be argumentative, arrogant and opinionated, which often helps in the rock music business. Yet he could also be kind and considerate. He shared his vast experience and understanding with many younger drummers and percussionists.

Powerhouse drummer Cozy Powell.

ALICE COOPER

From the name 'Alice Cooper', you might picture a quiet lady singing folksy ballads. Instead, you got a deafeningly heavy rock band, screams and wails, piercing guitar feedback, and an horrific stage show featuring zombies, axes, chainsaws and dripping blood. The lead singer even pretended to saw off his own arm or fry in his on-stage electric chair.

'Killer' January '72
'School's Out' July '72
'Billion Dollar Babies' March '73
'Welcome To My Nightmare' March '75
'Alice Cooper Goes To Hell' July '76
'Constrictor' October '86
'Trash' August '89
'The Last Temptation' June '94

FROM VINCENT TO ALICE

For 'Alice' was a he – Vincent Damon Furnier. At first the band was called Alice Cooper. They began as a reasonably successful heavy group, but by about 1970 they needed a kick-start. In came glam-horror, with ghoulish make-up, sinister lyrics about murder and mutilation, and a fright-a-minute stage act with snakes and other sinister symbols. There were reports of on-stage Alice beheading live chickens (actually fakes) and ripping blood-spurting limbs off toy dolls. Members of the audience fainted, vomited or walked out.

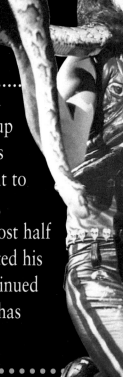

THEATRE, NOT MUSIC

But the shock tactics worked. After a low-20s hit in early 1972, the follow-up 'School's Out' made Top 5 in the albums chart, and the single of the same name went to No. 1. In 1973 the fourth album of this period, 'Billion Dollar Babies', was at No. 1 in the UK for almost half the year. In 1975, Furnier took the group's name for himself. Critics suggested his music needed the shock-horror theatrics for success. In reply, Alice has continued his themes and songs, though lately more tongue-in-cheek. In the 1990s he has broken into the Top 5 with several albums, including 1991's 'Hey Stoopid'.

CREAM

Cream were born out of the 'blues boom' in mid-1960s Britain. They took blues, made it into loud rock, added power chords, riffs and lengthy solos, and helped to forge the sound of heavy metal.

'Fresh Cream'
December '66
'Disraeli Gears'
November '67
'Wheels Of Fire' August '68

'Goodbye Cream' March '69
'Live Cream' June '70
'Strange Brew: Best Of Cream'
February '83

THE POWER TRIO

Cream's bassist Jack Bruce and drummer Ginger Baker came from jazz backgrounds, while blues fan Eric Clapton became the UK's first 'guitar hero' in John Mayall's Bluesbreakers. Clapton wanted to experiment and, impressed by their skills, invited Bruce and Baker to form a new style of band – the power trio. Cream was born in 1966.

TRIALS AND TENSIONS

The band's first album 'Fresh Cream' peaked at No. 5 in the UK album charts. A furious touring schedule ensued, but problems soon developed. Bruce and Baker had a history of arguments and even fist-fights. Yet on stage, these tensions seemed to help their music. The trio constantly extended and improvized their basic songs in the style of jazz musicians, with screaming notes from Clapton, Bruce playing bass like a lead guitar, and Baker developing 20-minute drum solos.

But it was very short-lived. Cream released seven singles and only three proper studio albums plus various 'live' versions. Thankfully their last concert at London's Albert Hall was captured on film. The inevitable split came on 26 November 1968 and left hordes of high-energy power-players heading towards true HM.

After Cream, Clapton (right) and Baker (centre-right) formed another 'supergroup', Blind Faith.

DEEP PURPLE

In April 1968, after intensive rehearsals in a Hertfordshire farmhouse, a new heavy band prepared to hit the road. But the members were cautious, and decided to debut away from the UK, in case they flopped. This is why Jon Lord, Ritchie Blackmore, Ian Paice, Rod Evans and Nick Simper played their first gig in a school hall in Tastrup, Denmark. Called Roundabout, the band soon changed its name. A heavy metal legend was born.

CLASSICAL AND ROCK

That first 11-date Danish tour was a modest success, and Deep Purple signed to Parlophone. Heavily influenced by American band Vanilla Fudge, their first two albums, 'Shades Of Deep Purple' and 'Book Of Taliesyn', featured extravagant re-workings of famous rock songs. Virtually ignored in the UK, they made the Top 10 in the USA. By 1969 guitarist Blackmore and keyboardist Lord were writing their own songs. Evans and Simper departed, replaced by vocalist Ian Gillan and bassist Roger Glover. After an unsteady rock-classical fusion 'Concerto For Group And Orchestra' came the HM classic, 'Deep Purple In Rock'. In 1970, the single 'Black Night' went to No. 2 in the UK.

'Shades Of Deep Purple' September '68
'Deep Purple In Rock' June '70
'Fireball' September '71
'Machine Head' April '72
'Made In Japan' December '72
'Burn' February '74

'Stormbringer' November '74
'Deep Purple Live' November '76
'Deepest Purple' (compilation) July '80
'Perfect Strangers' November '84
'The House Of Blue Light' January '87
'The Battle Rages On' July '93

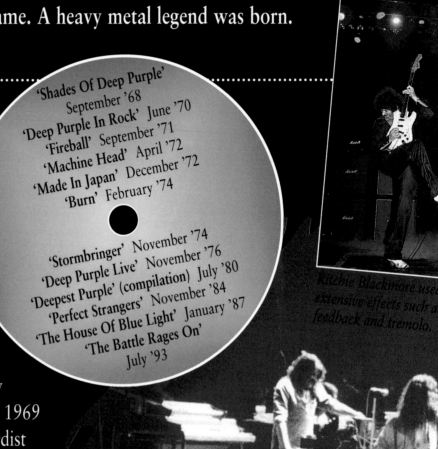

Ritchie Blackmore used extensive effects such as feedback and tremolo.

Purple line-up from left to right: Lord, Blackmore, Glover, Gillan and Paice.

The next two albums, 'Fireball' and 'Machine Head', both went one better. The latter included the enduring HM anthem with one of rock's most famous guitar riffs, 'Smoke On The Water'. However, egos clashed again. Gillan and Glover quit, replaced by singer David Coverdale – plucked from Lancashire obscurity – and bassist Glenn Hughes.

FADED PURPLE

In 1974 'Burn' and 'Stormbringer' made the Top 10, and Purple undertook massive world tours. But their direction and impetus were fading. In 1975 Blackmore left (see panel). In came jazz-influenced Tommy Bolin for the twelfth album, 'Come Taste The Band'. Tragically he died of drug abuse two years later. Gillan, Lord, Blackmore, Glover and Paice reformed Deep Purple in the 1980s, with some commercial success, but the original fire and energy were lacking. Ian Gillan was soon on his way once more. Despite their many changes, Deep Purple richly deserve their status as one of heavy metal's most exciting and innovative bands.

PURPLE SPIN-OFFS

Various members of Deep Purple have enjoyed post-Purple success. Pyrotechnic guitarist Ritchie Blackmore founded Rainbow, whose first album of that name made the Top 10 in 1975. His scorchingly fast style, featuring notes from strings bent almost beyond belief, has been imitated but never bettered. A bewildering number of musicians passed through Rainbow, and their 1986 compilation 'Finyl Album' reflects Blackmore's immense contribution to the heavy metal scene. Ian Gillan formed his own band Gillan, and also sang with Black Sabbath. In 1978 David Coverdale founded yet another long-lasting HM outfit, Whitesnake.

Rainbow featured Ronnie James 'Dio' on vocals.

GUNS N' ROSES

William Bailey, born in 1962 in Lafayette, Indiana, USA, started his performing career at the tender age of five – singing in his local church choir. However, the church's influence faded as Bailey became immersed in the loud, fast, exciting rock music broadcast by the USA's innumerable radio stations. In 1984 he teamed up with like-minded guitarist Jeffrey Isbell in Los Angeles. The two decided to form a band. First on the list were stage names. William and Jeffrey just would not do …

GETTING THE NAMES RIGHT

… So Bailey became Axl Rose, and Isbell re-titled himself Izzy Stradlin. With Tacii Guns on guitar and Rob Gardner on drums, they needed a band name. First it was Hollywood Rose, then LA Guns, but neither seemed quite right. In any case, Guns and Gardner left. Drummer Steven Adler joined, along with guitarist Saul Hudson, a native of Stoke-on-Trent, England. More name changes followed. Hudson became Slash, and the band became Guns N' Roses. With Duff McKagan on bass, 'Gee-En-Arr' hit the road with vengeance.

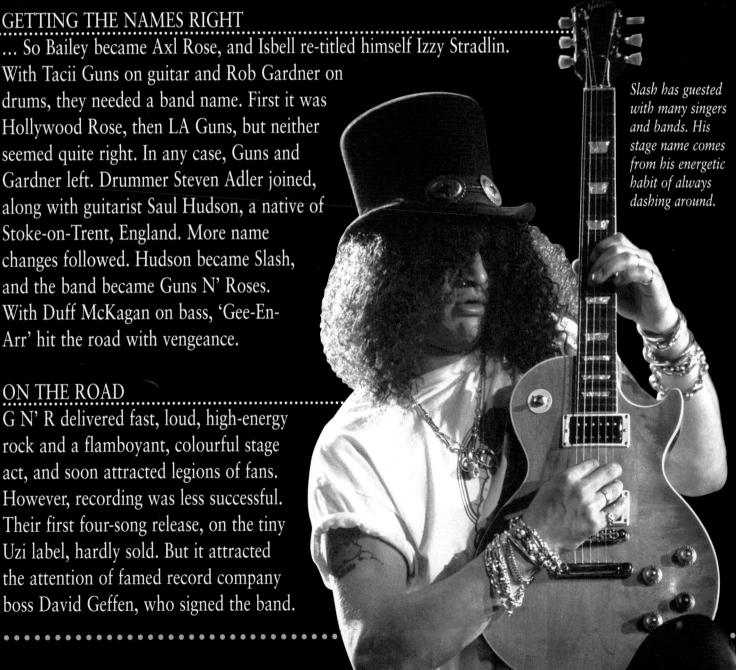

Slash has guested with many singers and bands. His stage name comes from his energetic habit of always dashing around.

ON THE ROAD

G N' R delivered fast, loud, high-energy rock and a flamboyant, colourful stage act, and soon attracted legions of fans. However, recording was less successful. Their first four-song release, on the tiny Uzi label, hardly sold. But it attracted the attention of famed record company boss David Geffen, who signed the band.

The first 'proper' album was 'Appetite For Destruction'. An apt title, since the band seemed bent on causing huge problems for themselves through drugs, alcohol, sexist and racist comments, swearing and generally offensive behaviour, which brought enormous and justified criticism. The first album took a year to reach No. 1 in the USA, although it has since sold more than 20 million copies. The next release was the live 'G N' R Lies…', which captured the band's electrifying stage performance. In 1990 further alcohol problems forced Adler to leave. He was replaced by Matt Sorum, with Izzy Stradlin still on rhythm guitar.

'Appetite
For Destruction'
July '87
'G N' R Lies …',
December '88

'Use Your Illusion I' and
'Use Your Illusion II'
September '91
'The Spaghetti Incident?'
November '93

W. Axl Rose cultivated his 'bad boy' image.

NUMBERS ONE AND TWO

However, there were positive signs. Slash's reputation as a highly skilled guitarist gained recording invitations from Michael Jackson and other respected performers. In 1991 'Use Your Illusion I' reached No. 2 – beaten to the top spot by its co-release 'Use Your Illusion II'. G N' R have gradually matured into one of HM's greatest acts.

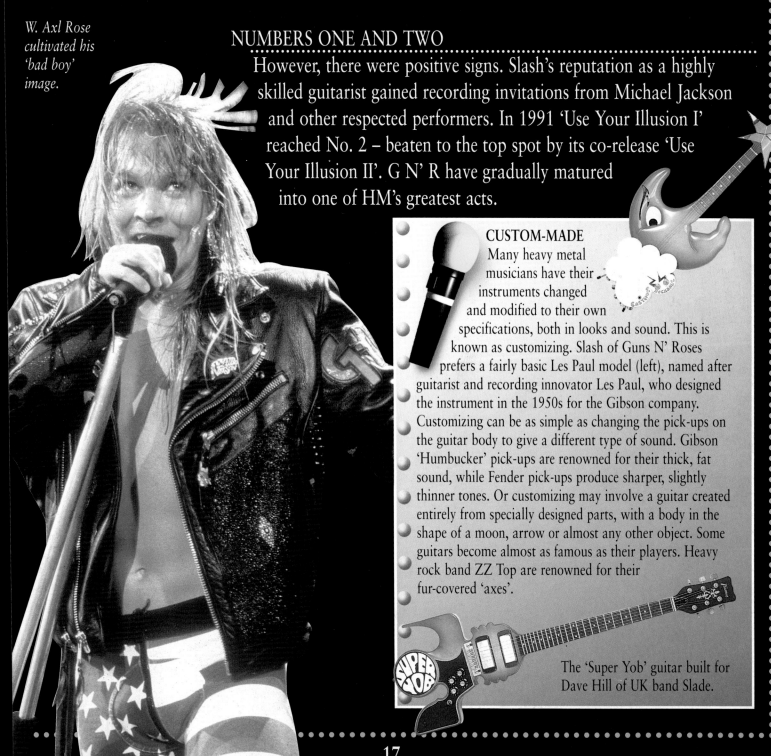

CUSTOM-MADE
Many heavy metal musicians have their instruments changed and modified to their own specifications, both in looks and sound. This is known as customizing. Slash of Guns N' Roses prefers a fairly basic Les Paul model (left), named after guitarist and recording innovator Les Paul, who designed the instrument in the 1950s for the Gibson company. Customizing can be as simple as changing the pick-ups on the guitar body to give a different type of sound. Gibson 'Humbucker' pick-ups are renowned for their thick, fat sound, while Fender pick-ups produce sharper, slightly thinner tones. Or customizing may involve a guitar created entirely from specially designed parts, with a body in the shape of a moon, arrow or almost any other object. Some guitars become almost as famous as their players. Heavy rock band ZZ Top are renowned for their fur-covered 'axes'.

The 'Super Yob' guitar built for Dave Hill of UK band Slade.

IRON MAIDEN

An 'iron maiden' was a body-shaped cage used in medieval times, to restrain and torture victims. Iron Maiden the band played its first gig much later, in 1976. Bassist Steve Harris recruited Paul Di'Anno on vocals, Dave Murray on guitar, and drummer Doug Samson.

CONTINUING CHANGES

Over the years, Iron Maiden has changed line-up regularly. The first album in 1980 saw Dennis Stratton on guitar and Clive Burr on drums. It reached No. 4 in the UK. Maiden worked hard to promote it, and three of its tracks made Top 40 singles. But Harris was still not convinced. For the next album, 'Killers', out went Stratton and in came Adrian Smith. British fans flocked to the band's gigs, but the USA took little notice.

NUMBER ONE, TIMES THREE

In 1980 Di'Anno left to form Lone Wolf. Sheffield-born Bruce Dickinson took over vocals, and the band had a Top 10 single 'Run To The Hills' and their first of three chart-topping albums, 'The Number Of The Beast'. At last, the USA also took notice. In 1983 drummer Nicko McBain replaced Burr. Maiden toured extensively and between 1983 and '90, six of their albums made the UK Top 10. After a break in 1988, guitarist Janick Gers replaced Adrian Smith. In 1993, Bruce Dickinson went solo. Yet more changes have not dented Iron Maiden's momentum, and the the band continues to hit the charts.

'Iron Maiden'
April '80
'The Number Of The Beast'
March '82
'Piece Of Mind' May '83
'Powerslave' September '84
'Somewhere In Time' September '86
'Seventh Son Of A Seventh Son' April '88
'Fear Of The Dark' May '92
'A Real Live One'
March '93

Steve Harris (left) is Maiden's founder member.

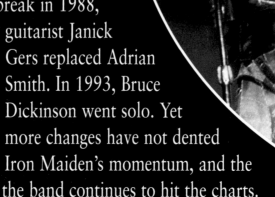

KISS

Kiss were outrageous and glamorous. The name refers to the act between romantic lovers. But written in capital letters, KISS, it stood for the band's approach to their music, as in: 'Keep It Simple, Stupid'.

'Destroyer' May '76
'Dynasty' June '79
'Creatures Of The Night' October '82
'Lick It Up' September '83

'Animalise' September '84
'Asylum' September '85
'Crazy Nights' October '87
'Revenge' May '92
'Alive III' May '93

WALKING TALL

In the early 1970s, 'glam rock' swept the modern music scene. Performers wore vivid make-up, glittering costumes and stack- or platform-soled boots. The trend spread to heavy metal, and one US band in particular took it to heart. They were Kiss, founded by bassist Gene Simmons (whose real name of Chaim Klein might seem more suited to the stage) and drummer Peter Criss.

KISS'S CRAZY NIGHTS

Kiss hit the charts with 'Destroyer' in 1976. Simmons took the stack-soled boots fashion to new heights – about 60 centimetres. After moderate successes, the 1983 album 'Lick It Up' achieved Top 10 status in the USA and UK. Kiss took their high-powered brand of glam-metal around the world on extensive tours.

In 1987 the album 'Crazy Nights' was another huge hit, while the single from it, 'Crazy Crazy Nights', has become a heavy rock classic.

LED ZEPPELIN

In the list of all-time greats in heavy music, Led Zeppelin would be near – or at – the top. They were born out of UK band the Yardbirds, whose line-ups had featured guitarists Eric Clapton and Jeff Beck.

Page and Plant (right) still perform in the '90s.

In 1968 bass player John Paul Jones joined the band and became friends with its guitarist of the time, Jimmy Page. The two decided to form a new group.

SECOND-CHOICE SINGER

Page and Jones' first choice for singer was Terry Reid. He was tied up by contracts, but he recommended the virtually unknown Robert Plant. He, in turn, suggested immensely powerful drummer John 'Bonzo' Bonham. The band name was provided by the Who's drummer, Keith Moon, who joked that they would 'go down like a lead (leaden) zeppelin', referring to the famous, ill-fated, German airships.

SPEEDY SUCCESS

Lead became Led, and the quartet signed with Peter Grant, a manager with a fearsome reputation. As musicians, the band were already experienced.

'Led Zeppelin'
March '69
'Led Zeppelin II'
October '69
'Led Zeppelin III' October '70
'Led Zeppelin IV' November '71
'Houses Of The Holy' April '73

'Physical Graffiti' March '75
'Presence' April '76
'The Song Remains The Same' (live) October '76
'Remasters' (compilation)
October '90
'Boxed Set II' (compilation)
October '93

The first album with a Zeppelin airship.

Jimmy Page was a veteran of dozens of recordings, including Van Morrison's, as an anonymous 'session guitarist'. Jones had played with ex-Shadow Tony Meehan, and also with Plant in the Birmingham-based Band Of Joy. But the sheer speed of Led Zep's success surprised everyone. The first album in March 1969, released on the huge Atlantic label, shot into the Top 10 in Europe and the USA. It featured Page's stunning, blues-influenced playing, Plant's tortured vocals, Jones' solid bass and organ work and Bonham's massive drumming. Just eight months later, 'Led Zeppelin II' topped charts around the world. It re-defined heavy rock music and is often quoted as the first true, riff-laden, heavy metal album. Zeppelin toured continually in their customized Boeing jetliner, performing spell-binding shows all over the world. Their anthem, the blues-rooted 'Whole Lotta Love', was re-recorded by CCS and became the signature tune of the UK's long running TV show, 'Top Of The Pops'.

The second album has the band members 'pasted' into the photograph.

STAIRWAY TO GREATNESS

By 1971 Led Zeppelin were demonstrating a more subtle, delicate approach. The album often referred to as Led Zep 4 or Symbols, but with the official title of four squiggle-like runes (ancient symbols), includes one of rock's greatest works. 'Stairway to Heaven' begins with acoustic guitar and recorder. Zeppelin's second to sixth albums went straight to No. 1 in the UK and USA, a feat equalled by few others. 1976's 'The Song Remains The Same' concert at New York's Madison Square Gardens captured the band on film. However on Christmas Day 1980, John Bonham died after a drinking session. Zeppelin immediately disbanded, although Page and Plant have revisited their music in the 1990s.

MASTERS OF THE RIFF

Led Zeppelin, like many heavy metal and heavy rock bands, based their songwriting around riffs. A riff is a fairly short sequence of notes which is repeated many times through the song. The openings of Zep's 'Whole Lotta Love' and Metallica's 'Enter Sandman' are classic examples. The riff is usually played by the guitarist, and perhaps keyboardist, and often by the bassist too, for that 'heavy' sound. It may be extended and developed in middle sections of the song, then re-stated in the closing sections. In a band with two on-stage guitarists, one may play the basic riff, while the other chooses notes in harmony and improvizes around it.

Page with twin-necked guitar (6 and 12 strings).

METALLICA

In 1981, Danish-born drummer Lars Ulrich and local guitarist-vocalist James Hetfield placed almost identical adverts in a Los Angeles music paper. Each wanted a 'soul mate', a like-minded partner to develop a new metal band which would have the heaviest sound of all time. The two got together, clicked at once, and even agreed on the name for their new group.

A SHARED VISION

Hetfield and Ulrich began the search for band members to share their ideas. Ron McGovney joined on bass, but first guitarist Lloga Grand was quickly replaced by David Mustaine. By 1982 Mustaine also left, to develop his own career with thrash-metal band Megadeth. The next year, Cliff Burton came in as bassist. With Kirk Hammett on lead guitar, Ulrich and Hetfield were at last beginning to achieve the sound they wanted.

'Ride The Lightning'
July '84
'Master Of Puppets'
March '86
'And Justice For All'
September '88
'The Good, The Bad And The Live' May '90

'Metallica' (black album)
August '91
'Live Sh*t — Binge And Purge'
December '93
'Reload'
November '97

SUCCESS AND DISASTER

Metallica moved to the US East Coast and John Zazula's Mega Force label. The first albums, in 1984 and '86, caused few waves. But the band persevered, honing their extravagant and incredibly loud stage show.

Their songs were immensely powerful, dark and brooding, and drew musical comparisons with Black Sabbath. In 1986 'Master Of Puppets' broke into the Top 50. It seemed that five years of hard work were paying off at last. But in September '86, on tour in Sweden, the band bus crashed and bassist Cliff Burton died. Hetfield and Ulrich were tempted to finish, there and then. But they came around to the opinion that Burton would have wanted them to continue.

Cartoon heroes Beavis and Butthead are devoted Metallica fans.

THE BLACK ALBUM

Metallica recruited Jason Newsted on bass. He did not try to copy his predecessor Burton, but brought his own voice, songwriting ideas and style of playing. In 1988, 'And Justice For All' broke into the Top 10 album charts in the USA and UK. In 1991 the band struck gold, or rather, black. The black cover of the album 'Metallica', with the snake logo in dark silver, meant that this recording is known simply as the 'black album' (a great honour, derived from the Beatles' 'white album'). It made No. 1 in the USA, UK and most of Europe.

Lead guitarist Hammett (above) and main singer Hetfield (left).

BENDING THE RULES

Metallica went on to bend and even break a few HM rules. They featured delicate harmonies and quiet passages. Their lyrics showed an open-minded, caring approach. They wrote protest songs against political and social injustice, while many other heavy bands refused to condemn such problems. In 1991, Metallica's storming performance at Donington's Monsters of Rock festival cemented their reputation as one of heavy metal's most thrilling, innovative, and LOUD bands.

IN THE STUDIO

Heavy metal is sometimes seen as a simple wham-crash-thud type of music. But for most HM bands, nothing could be further from the truth.

Metallica's founders, Ulrich and Hetfield, could hear the distinctive sound they wanted in their heads. But it took several changes of band membership to come close. A final piece of the jigsaw was record producer Bob Rock. His sympathetic ear and wide experience helped to knit together the deep guitar and bass riffs and pounding drums, into one of HM's weightiest sounds.

The recording studio, where a band's 'sonic signature' is developed.

MOTORHEAD

Colourful characters abound in heavy metal. After all, the music itself is larger than life, with its sheer power and intensity, and sometimes aggressive style. HM is rarely used as background music for a quiet dinner party! And characters are rarely more colourful than Motorhead's founder, bassist and singer, Lemmy.

A SHAKY BEGINNING

Ian Kilmister was born on Christmas Eve 1945, in Stoke-on-Trent, England – the son of a vicar. His nickname, Lemmy, came from his frequent pleas for money loans: 'Lemme (lend me) a fiver!' Once a roadie for Jimi Hendrix, Lemmy was bass player in hippie-rock band Hawkwind from 1971. In 1975 he was sacked after drug charges and keen for revenge, he formed his own band to play heavier, faster rock. The band name is slang for a person who takes amphetamine drugs ('speed').

FAST AND ANIMAL

After a false start with Larry Wallis and Lucas Fox, Lemmy's casual friend Phil 'Animal' Taylor – limited experience but the right image – became his drummer. The power trio format was completed by experienced guitarist 'Fast' Eddie Clarke. Motorhead would certainly not achieve overnight success. And they have never made a dent in the US album or singles charts.

'Motorhead'
August '77
'Overkill' March '79
'Bomber' October '79
'Ace Of Spades' October '80
'No Sleep Til Hammersmith' June '81
'Ironfist' April '82

'Another Perfect Day' May '83
'No Remorse' (compilation)
September '84
'Orgasmatron' July '86
'1916' January '91

But their frantic, energetic and sometimes deafening performances steadily built up large, enthusiastic audiences. In August 1977 their first album scraped into the UK Top 50. Three singles sold modestly and Motorhead's reputation slowly grew. In 1979 they made the UK Top 30 with the aptly named 'Overkill'.

FINALLY NUMBER ONE

In October the same year, the third album 'Bomber' peaked at No. 12. Each release fared better until the band's second live album, 'No Sleep Til Hammersmith', made No. 1. The 1980 single 'Ace of Spades', from the same-name album, has become a metal classic. In 1982 Clarke went off to form Fastway. Ex-Thin Lizzy guitarist Brian Robertson (see page 26) stepped in. However the success of 'Hammersmith' was never recaptured.

THE 'TAP' ON TOUR

Heavy metal often seems to make fun of itself. Performers totter about on huge-heeled shoes, with theatrical stage make-up and extravagantly customized guitars. The fairground feel and tacky showmanship contribute to the sheer fun of it all. However in 1984 an achingly amusing film, 'This Is Spinal Tap', provided the ultimate spoof on heavy rock. It is a fictional account of distinctly fading band, Spinal Tap, and it sends up all aspects of the rock world. Ridiculously inflated egos, stupidly grandiose ideas, crooked managers, awful songwriting and dreadful record deals conspire to bring disaster at every turn. Like all good satire, the fiction is only slightly removed from the reality. Spinal Tap even turned themselves into a real band and toured to promote their spoof (but excellent) album 'Break The Wind'.

Actors turned heavy rockers of Spinal Tap.

In 1983 Robertson left. Guitarist Michael Burston, nicknamed 'Wurzel' because of his resemblance to the children's fictional favourite, scarecrow-tramp Wurzel Gummidge, joined Phil Cambell and Lemmy. Taylor moved on, and drummer Pete Gill moved in. Lemmy thought another live album might provide a boost, but 1988's 'No Sleep At All' only managed to scrape into the Top 100. Original drummer Taylor returned and, through the 1990s, Motorhead have continued their full-tilt approach – still one of British

THIN LIZZY

Thin Lizzy began in Dublin in 1969 – the brainchild of lanky, exotic-looking bass player and singer, Phil Lynott. Guitar player Eric Bell and drummer Brian Downey completed the trio. Phil had previously played in another Irish outfit, Skidrow. They were led by a 16-year old guitar star who would later achieve international fame, and be part of Thin Lizzy for a time. His name was Gary Moore.

MELODY TO METAL

Thin Lizzy started as a distinctly non-heavy band, playing a melodic mix of songs which reflected Lynott's Irish-Brazilian parentage. By 1972, the trio had two interesting but unsuccessful Decca albums behind them. Then came their tuneful but strong single 'Whiskey In The Jar'. It echoed their increasingly forceful direction, due in no small part to Lynott's powerful stage presence. It entered the UK Top 10 in January 1973, peaked at No. 6, and is still heard regularly. Lizzy moved further into heavy metal land, but the third album did not match the single's success. 1974 saw a succession of changes. Bell left and in came Phil Lynott's old Skidrow chum, Gary Moore. Not for long.

'Jailbreak'
March '76
'Johnny The Fox' October '76
'Bad Reputation' September '77
'Live And Dangerous'
June '78
'Black Rose' April '79
'Chinatown' October '80

'Adventures Of Thin Lizzy' April '81
'Renegade' November '81
'Thunder And Lightning' March '83
'Life' November '83
'Dedication: The Very Best Of Thin Lizzy'
February '91

The band regained its balance when Lynott took on Scott Gorham and Brian Robertson as twin lead guitarists. A lengthy tour of the UK enhanced Thin Lizzy's reputation as one of the more imaginative heavy bands. 1975's album 'Fighting' was a minor hit, but the next one was massive. 'Jailbreak' reached No. 10 in the UK and stayed in the album chart for a year. In May 1976 the single 'The Boys Are Back In Town' went four places better – and also made the Top 20 in the USA.

Phil 'Johnny the Fox' Lynott's heavy rock songs had romantic, folksy influences.

LIVE AND DANGEROUS

In 1977, Brian Robertson was forced to take time out with a hand injury. Back came Gary Moore. The album 'Bad Reputation' got to No. 4, and the following 'Live And Dangerous' (1978), one of heavy rock's classic live performances, reached No. 2. However, bewildering personnel changes continued. Robertson left again; Moore returned again. In September 1979 he was replaced by guitarist Midge Ure from Ultravox. In turn, he was replaced by Snowy White. Out came the excellent album 'Chinatown', and the single of the same name gave Thin Lizzy their first No. 1. 'Adventures Of Thin Lizzy', a compilation album, was yet another hit, but membership changes followed.

AN EARLY LOSS

'Thunder And Lightning' was released in 1983 and reached No. 4. However, in 1984 Phil Lynott decided that his band had run its course. He dissolved Thin Lizzy. Tragically, just two years later, he was dead. A charming and enigmatic man, and an intelligent song-crafter, Lynott sadly succumbed to drugs and alcohol addiction. He was just 35 years old.

DRUMS GALORE

Vocalists and guitarists often dominate the stage shows of heavy metal bands. Drummers are hidden behind their huge kits, unable to pose or rush about. Yet loud, solid drumming is the backbone of heavy rock. Rick Allen of Def Leppard is a fine example, but with a difference. He lost one arm in an accident. However, his specially customized kit enables him to carry on playing. Def Leppard have enjoyed more success in the USA than in their native UK.

Def Leppard are from Sheffield, England.

VAN HALEN

The riverside town of Nijmegen in Holland is the birthplace of two of the best-known heavy metal performers, Eddie (guitar) and Alex (drums) Van Halen. The brothers emigrated to the USA in the 1960s.

BORN TO ROCK

The Van Halen boys loved rock music, and teamed up with Chicago-born bass player Michael Antony and singer David Lee Roth, as Mammoth. Right from the start, they put everything into their loud, powerful, uncompromising metal music, performing in any Los Angeles venue, no matter how small. In the audience one night was Gene Simmons of Kiss (see page 19). He was impressed, especially with David Lee Roth's singing, and decided to help. But the name Mammoth was already taken by another band. After dismissing Rat Salade, the band decided that they would be known simply as Van Halen. Simmons introduced them to producer Ted Templeman, who quickly signed them to Warner Brothers. Van Halen's first album, released in early 1978, entered the Top 40 on both sides of the Atlantic. Over the following year it sold more than two million copies around the world.

THE HEAVY BASS

One of the defining sounds of heavy metal music is the low notes of the bass guitar, often thudding in time to the bass drum. The bassist can repeat the basic notes of the key, for a solid, unfussy foundation to the song, or follow the notes of the other guitarists to emphasize the riffs. Playing bass may seem an easy option, compared to a frontman vocalist or guitarist. But the bassist must stay in perfect synchrony with the drummer, or the bedrock of the HM sound loses its kick and punch.

Rick Savage plays bass in Def Leppard.

The success of Van Halen was due partly to David Lee Roth's stunning singing and outrageous stage presence. He captivated audiences with his wild-man antics and over-the-top performances. More importantly, his vocals also sounded great in the more demanding environment of the recording studio, where small variations in tone and key become far more obvious. In 1978, Eddie Van Halen was named as Best New Guitarist by the influential American magazine, 'Guitar Player'. But the band's early singles did less well. They had to wait until the release of their second album, in April 1979, before their fifth single made the Top 20 in the USA.

'Van Halen'
April '78
'Van Halen II' April '79
'Women And Children First' March '80
'Fair Warning' May '81
'Diver Down' May '82
'1984' January '84

'5150' March '86
'OU812' June '88
'Live: Right Here, Right Now'
February '93
'Balance' January '95
'Van Halen III' March '98

David Lee Roth had a hit solo album in 1991 with 'A Little Ain't Enough'.

JUMPING INTO THE CHARTS

In 1979 the group's spectacular rise to fame moved into top gear. 'Van Halen II' sold better than their first album. The momentum continued for six years, with four more Top 50 albums. Only five of their 13 singles cracked the Top 20. But one was 'Jump' – their first No. 1. The album that carried it, '1984', stayed in US Billboard charts for a year. However, in 1985 the band reverted to a trio when dynamic David Lee Roth left to try his luck solo. Next year a new singer appeared – Sammy Hagar from HM band Montrose. The first single featuring Hagar went to No. 3 in the USA. The album '5150' (which is the US police code for prisoners considered insane) became their first of four US No. 1s, although it only reached No. 16 in the UK. Van Halen have continued to enjoy world success, filling huge stadiums with their extravagant, exciting stage shows. Eddie Van Halen also made an impressive guest appearance on one of the biggest-selling albums of all time, Michael Jackson's 1982 'Thriller'.

GAZETTEER

Since the 1960s, heavy metal music has diversified into many different forms. A book like this cannot detail the hundreds of top-class 'heavy' performers through the years. Selected bands shown here demonstrate the many styles of heavy rock music.

The Gibbons brothers of ZZ Top.

HEAVY BOOGIE

The term 'heavy rock' includes a wide variety of loud, energetic music styles, featuring mainly guitar, bass guitar and drums, and perhaps keyboards. Texan band ZZ Top play 'heavy metal boogie', based around the 12-bar blues format widely used in boogie and rock 'n' roll. Their 1983 album 'Eliminator', with their trademark red custom car, sold millions. In the 1970s, British group Nazareth also played a basic rock beat with plentiful slide guitar. They had a Top 10 album, 'Loud 'n' Proud', in 1973.

HEAVY ROCK

More varied and theatrical is the music of Meatloaf. Working with acclaimed record producer and

Meatloaf's original name was Marvin Lee Aday.

songwriter Jim Steinman, his recordings have long songs with many different sections, changing in pace and rhythm and featuring piano passages, trumpets and even violins. His massive seller 'Bat Out Of Hell', released in 1978, has spent a total of nine years in the Top 100 album chart. The follow-up 'Bat Out Of Hell II – Back Into Hell' reached No. 1 in 1993.

Another hugely successful band are Rush, from Canada. They had six Top 10 albums in the 1980s.

Rush hit the big time with 'Permanent Waves' in 1980.

Their style is loud and heavy, yet melodic. The tunes are catchy and some have a quieter, more romantic feel. This type of music, with a wider appeal, is termed AOR, adult-orientated rock. One of AOR's most popular performers is former recording studio tea-boy, Jon Bon Jovi. He is leader-singer-songwriter-guitarist in the band that bears his name. Since 'New Jersey' in 1988, each Bon Jovi album has reached No. 1. Jon has also written movie soundtracks such as 'Young Guns II'.

Nazareth's 1973 single 'Broken Down Angel' made the UK Top 10.

GRUNGE

A new type of heavy music appeared in about 1990. Known as grunge, it is weighty but generally fairly slow, with a scowling, grinding feel, very distorted guitar sounds, growled vocals and angry lyrical content. Widely successful grunge bands include Seattle-based Nirvana, whose 1991 album 'Nevermind' helped to define the sound, and Smashing Pumpkins. Sadly Nirvana's vocalist-guitarist Kurt Cobain shot himself in 1994 in a fit of deep depression.

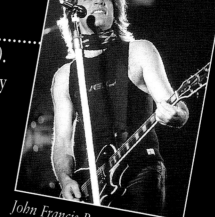

John Francis Bongiovi Junior – alias Jon Bon Jovi.

OTHER 'METALS'

There are many other kinds of metal-based heavy music. Thrash metal is played almost excessively fast. Death metal, whose performers include Brazilian band Sepultura, is obsessed with dying, skulls, skeletons, coffins and graveyards. No doubt other exciting, energetic 'metals' will appear in future years.

Smashing Pumpkins

Sepultura write about social issues in their homeland.

31

INDEX

PHOTOGRAPHIC CREDITS *Abbreviations: t-top, m-middle, b-bottom, r-right, l-left, c-centre*
Front cover c & br, 6bl, 7l, 8tl, 14m, 18-19, 21b, 22 & 29b - E. Reberts/Redferns. Cover bl, 7r, 9m, 11 both, 14t, 19 both, 24tl, 26t, 26-27, 27t, 28t, 29t, 30b & 31t - F. Costello/Redferns. Cover bm, 3, 6m, 8bl, 8-9, 12t & br, 16b, 18b, 25l, 27b, 28br, 30t, 31mr & b - M. Hutson/Redferns. 4-5 & 12bl - R. Aaron/Redferns. 5tl - E. Echenberg/Redferns. 6tl & 31ml P. Ford/Redferns. 10t - Gems/Redferns. 10m - S. Ritter/Redferns. 10b, 14-15 & 15t - A. Putler/Redferns. 13t - C. Stewart/Redferns. 13m - K. Morris/Redferns. 13b - Michael Ochs Archive/Redferns. 15b, 21tl & tr & 30m - Redferns. 20t - T. Hanley/Redferns. 20b - I. Dickson. 23t - Frank Spooner Pictures. 22-23 - G. DeSota/Redferns. 23m - M. Linssen/Redferns. 23b - S. Gibbons/Redferns. 24m - P. Cronin. 25r - Embassy Films (courtesy Kobal Collection).